How I Met Van and Numan

Future, Present and Past

How I Met Van and Numan

Future, Present and Past

by

Steve Brooks

How I Met Van and Numan
Future, Present and Past
A Buns on Mars book
All rights reserved
Copyright © 2013
bunsonmars.com

Contents:

Chapter 1 Chairman Le Jour's Office, Mars - Future - 2742	page 1
Chapter 2 C.L.O.D. Orbiter - Present	page 21
Chapter 3 Earth - Past	page 36
Chapter 4 Earth Apartment - Present	page 47
Chapter 5 Earth - Past	page 65
Chapter 6 Chairman Le Jour's Office - Future	page 87
Chapter 7 Mars - Past	page 124
Chapter 8 The Red Sun's Zenith Club - Present	page 145
Chapter 9 Chairman Das Nacht's Office - Future	page 165

To Roberta Brooks, consultant
Eliott Brooks, front cover design
Paul Brooks, consultant
Fred Zinos, encouragement

How I Met Van and Numan

Future, Present and Past

by Steve Brooks

Chapter 1
Chairman Le Jour's Office, Mars
Future
2742

"Suzette? Suzette? Can you hear me? This intercom is on the fritz again! Can you fix it? Suzette! Are you there?"

"Sorry, Chairman Le Jour. I was sharpening all your pencils for your meeting. You need to be prepared. I can't sit by and let you solely rely on your ESP."

"Please send in General George Keith."

"Moon-mo-men-to, Chairman Le Jour."

"Can I go in now, sweetheart? I heard what he said and..."

"Ooops, there goes another tip, won't have to resharpen that one!"

"Girl? I've been waiting forty five minutes here. If you don't send me in right now, I will part the back of your hair with both of my hands and ride you like a spring pony."

"Well sir, don't have a cow! Go right in."

"Good morning, Chairman Le Jour, sir."

"Aaah, George, come right in, have a seat."

"Quite a receptionist you've got there. I've been watching her by the water cooler in that low cut blouse of hers. She's a real Poser. I should come over here more often. Great view you have. These civilian offices come with real perks. A real step up from the barracks."

"Thanks, George. Glad you like it. You can stop staring out the door now. Please close it and focus on our meeting."

"So, I suppose you're expecting my weekly progress report on the battle lines with the Chinese Martians. Well, let me say something about that. It's always shifting and it's always dusty out there. It's hard to keep track on the status of hundreds of clones, all Generations, from either side getting lost. I've had a real headache with our new filing cabinets – drawers always getting stuck. Plus, I've been working out a new landscaping geometry, using rocks as borders. With my new system, all the barracks look like they have neat lawns. I could do the same for the Institute, here, if you wanted? It would make the place look so homey. Honestly, I really don't know how the week flies by. I'm so racked with work duties, my back is to the wall, sir. I really don't have the time."

"I didn't call you into my office for that nonsense, but now that you mentioned it, I do expect to see a progress report on my desk, by the end of the day."

"Dang. I will try, I promise."

"Very well, then. Shall we begin? I called you into my office to discuss a new assignment for you. All the other Generals are too busy playing golf, or on vacation, so that leaves you, unfortunately."

"That's not good, sir. I mean, too bad."

"Have you heard of the Valhalla Project?"

"No, sir. I haven't"

"Good! We try our utmost to keep certain things from the military."

"We should be in the dark, sir, half of the time, sir."

"Have you looked up at the night skies lately?"

"I really can't recall at the moment."

"So, you haven't noticed that Mars has a ring of debris around it?"

"To the best of my recollection, I can't say whether or not, at this time. I mean, to the best of my knowledge, it hasn't occurred to me over all in my mind to bother watching the stars this past week or the week after, or to read the paper about that issue. I really don't know which one?"

"Cut the crap. I expected this from you."

"What's that, sir?"

"Unless you've been living in a hole in the ground or haven't noticed bad television reception?"

"I have been landscaping with rocks, sir, – around the barracks, that is."

"For months now, we've observed a huge asteroid coming at us, we called Thor's Hammer. It skidded on Phobos, bounced off Deimos, and finally slammed into another Martian satellite, scattering debris along our thermosphere. We look like Saturn now, and we can't have *that* aura! What will Earth say? They'll get confused. So, we've been looking into some solutions. The Valhalla Project is our best strategy to deal with this mess. I was talking to Philip the other day..."

"Who is Philip?"

"Chairman Das Nacht, you idiot!"

"Sorry, I don't get over here too often."

"Well, Philip came up with the kooky idea of creating a orbital hurricane machine to blow the debris away from Mars. I wasn't too keen on this idea at the time, until a few nights ago. I had a dream. I dreamed I was walking the streets of Paris, not too far from where I grew up. I noticed all these beautiful colors falling around me. When I reached out my hand, to catch a drop of color, I realized it was a falling leaf. I heard my mother calling me home for dinner. I turned around, and saw a street sweeper vacuuming all the different colors, splattered in the street. I immediately woke up, and wrote down my ideas. At first, I thought it was a Freudian thing, then I thought - Jungian. I couldn't make up my mind. But then I thought about Philip and his wacky hurricane machine, and it occurred to me at that moment. I envisioned an unmanned space craft with a special armature, that collects the debris of Thor's Hammer. The ship will send down the raw materials to the Institute, where we will sort through the minerals, especially the silver and gold, for minting commemorative I Ching coins, or merely, for desk legs, pens, and other school supplies."

"A brilliant idea, sir. If I may say so."

"Oh, you may. I extra-sensed it was. It will benefit all of mankind. It will be the greatest wonder since the NASA space shuttle, only for Mars!"

"Indeed, so, sir. Are we finished here?"

"No, not by any means. Our Class O2 Debris Hardware ship or C.L.O.D. Recycling orbiter is nearly finished and ready for take off. It's all there, except for the minor decisions of appropriating storage and living space. This is a matter of approving where we're going to put the Repair Personal living quarters, computers, and what level we're putting the warehouse for the second phase of ship regeneration. And that is the whole genius of the thing. Not only, will the ship recycle debris from Thor's Hammer and old satellites, it will collect and construct materials to recycle the ship itself. It will be a perpetual system of recycling and construction, fueled by the trash of space."

"Wow, sir. Quite an ambiguous project!"

"Unfortunately, other overhead costs with the Institute have forced me to re-evaluate my role in the Valhalla Project. The primary expense, as informed to me by an accounts auditor, Mr. Henry Farnsworth, is our massive tea imports, which we use in our Tea Leaf Reading courses. It seems, we bought too much of the wrong tea. The teas we imported from the American Federation are not adequate for Tea Leaf Reading. Our Tea Leaf Reading students were getting lower grade point averages. The American tea leaves are longer and curl around, forming English letters. We'll have to return all of that product and import real Chinese tea. One that forms Chinese characters in the bottoms of our exam tea cups. You probably get an idea of how bogged down I am with this. It will be expensive to adjust, it will take a while for the grade points to swing back up, and I'll be too busy with my other duties to supervise the rest of the Valhalla Project."

"So, this is why you brought me into your office today, sir?"

"In some ways, yes. I am handing over part of my duties to you. Your only responsibility will be the scheduling of the remaining maintenance of the orbiter – things like sweeping, tool rental returns, and payroll card collection. This will lead up to your final duties with the scheduling of the blast off."

"I am quite amazed and honored with this responsibility, Chairman Sir."

"Good. Glad to hear you'll be earnest and focused with your work. Now, I must place special emphasis here. This will be an unmanned orbiter. Got that? We can put a maintenance crew up there for only a couple of days each semester, due to our budget costs. The orbiter's function will be strictly ecological, cleaning up the thermosphere, for the good of Mars. None of the materials sent down will be used for building rovers, ammunition, or anything else, associated with our ongoing covert war with the Chinese. They're very touchy, suspicious, and think we always want to borrow from them. They even get mad when we ask *them* to pick up *their* own trash! I know that some of it's ours, but still, they holler at us for any little thing that gets blown over the red line. We have to keep them out of the loop to avoid asking questions. So, repeat after me. It will be an unmanned mission."

"Gosh, do I have to?"

"If I hear you've altered this mission in any way for personal or military gain, you can kiss your rank, serial number, and benefits, goodbye. Now, say it."

"Alright. It will be an unmanned shuttle, I mean, orbiter. What I'm really trying to state is the mission won't have any human involvement. It simply won't have anything humanly possible."

"George?!! Say it."

"Okaaay! It will be an un**man**ned mission for non-humans."

"Very well, then. If you keep the project on track, I expect to see the Milky Way and Earth through my telescope, as well as having good television reception, by the end of the year. Are we clear on that?"

"I'll certainly try my best, sir. I already have two Seventh Generation clones, who sit on their ass all day, in mind to do clean up duty."

"Good! You keep their ass in mind. I suggest you get all of your shit in a pile. You're gonna need it. Our meeting is done. Good day, General."

"Thanks again for this, I'll do my best. Good day, Chairman Le Jour. Oh, by the way, sir?"

"What's that?"

"I was wondering? May I speak to Suzette on my way out?"

"No, I'd rather you not. She's a work in progress. I haven't re-set her Clone Dome values or read her mind yet. She's much too distracted as it is. I might fire her."

"Fire her? She's a doll faced doll. Why would you let her go?"

"Oh, I think she might do better over at the ESP office. She doesn't think she has to do anything."

"Well, she's certainly a piece of work, if I may say so."

"You should pay attention to your own distractions, General. You should get going with your new assignment. I want to see the results, and soon..."

Thah-wang!

"10 zip. Game, set, and match. I win again."

"Well, I protest. I didn't sense that one coming. I wasn't ready."

"Snooze, you lose."

"You were too close when you threw it. You stepped over the line."

"How can you tell?"

"Affirmative. I measured the velocity of the volleyball, to the depth of the dent it left in my modem panel, to the angle of ricochet, and how you were about four feet away when you whipped it at me."

"Good one, Puter, but *come on.* I won ten matches in a row. Can't you try a little bit harder? It really gets boring when I win all the time."

"Affirmative. I understand. Perhaps you might connect me to a robot armature that has wheels and arms. Then, I'll be able to move and return the ball to you. I can also sense by your language that you really don't like shagging the ball."

"That's a good idea, Puter. I hadn't thought of that."

"Just doing my job, Van."

"Puter? You've always been real to me since they assigned us together, but there are certain things that just don't add up?"

"Affirmative?"

"Like, I've always been hungry ever since I can remember. I really get hungry after we throw the ball, and this white noise is always in the background, but the white noise is in every module. It's everywhere, and I am hungry all the time. So, what's up with all that?"

"Negative? I can't process your statement. You must put it in the form of a question."

"Okay, Puter. Does the white noise make me hungry?"

"Affirmative? Seventh Generation clones are bio-engineered to be hungry all the time for manipulation purposes. The constant white noise is from the life support system machines. While you throw the ball, the white noise machines keeps you alive, and you will always be hungry."

"So, if I am not hungry, does the white noise stop?"

"Negative. The consuming of food doesn't affect the white noise. In fact, it doesn't give a crab apple if you live or die. If the white noise really bothers you, you can get a helmet with ear phones, and if you don't throw the ball so hard at me, denting my panels, you won't get so hungry."

"Are you telling me that you don't want to play throw the ball anymore?"

"Negative. I really enjoy our time together."

"Will you try harder next time?"

"Affirmative. You can use me as a goal post or back wall anytime you'd like. Okay?"

"Alright then, if I understand this white noise deal, I must chow down at the Module 16 dispensary, on the third floor."

"Affirmative. Can I go along this time?"

"Well, Puter, I don't know? It's a hassle to bring along a little Puter all the time. The Second Generation clones will laugh at me."

"Oh, I won't be a tag-along. Just fold me up like it's your very own laptop, and look important, like they do. They won't know the difference..."

"Hey, Van!"

"Hey, DeWayne."

"I know something you don't know."

"Oh, yeah? What?"

"Brown stucco."

"What's that?"

"It's when you step in shit-gummo."

"Hardy-har-har, De*Wayne*. So funny I forgot to laugh - I'll have to do-do that later."

"Speaking of his royal shit, I know something you don't know."

"What's that, DeWayne?"

"I'll tell you, if you buy me a peanut flavored 596 energy bar."

"For that? *It* better be good!"

"Oh, it's choice."

"Okay, then, cough it up, pronto."

"Saw General George Keith, walking around, hollering for you. Weren't you absent again today? I think you're in big trouble. You better hide."

"Like I didn't know. DeWayne."

"No problem. I'll expect a fully wrapped, not partly eaten, peanut flavored 596 energy bar, waiting for me, in my locker, by tomorrow. And it better be there, chump, or I'll tell General Keister that you were playing throw the ball at your little computer, during office hours."

"You're such a little rat tattle tale, DeWayne. Why can't you be just a regular Eighth Generation, like the rest of your class?"

"Who can be regular with the shit they feed us - when I got Seventh Generation dorks like you to buy me stuff?"

"One of these days, DeWayne, we ain't gonna fall for your scams. What then?"

"Not a chance, you guys are simple."

"Hey, where are you going?"

"I gotta skate and catch the Third Generation Girl's gym showers. I heard they're changing in Module 87 today. You should come along."

"I'm not falling for that one. You'll probably lead me right into General Keith."

"That's your loss. Catch you later, Van."

"Catch you later, DeWayne. Say Puter? How long have I worked in the supply clerk's office?"

"Affirmative, about 10 weeks now."

"And what did I do before that?"

"Imitation lawn mowing."

"And what did I do before that?"

"Trash inspection and sorting."

"And what did I do before that?"

"Hang work notices."

"Wasn't that all for General George Keith?"

"Affirmative."

"Doesn't that rat bastard owe me *something*?"

"Union pay distribution for Seventh Generation clones is a rather complicated mess. Percentages are made from the Martian Federation, the Martian Army, and the Edgar Cayce Institute, but are then deducted for eating, sleeping, and entertainment allowances. Each wage or deduction is appropriated from each institute, depending on the economy. One hand washes the other, in a manner of speaking, to keep each other in debt, so that no one really knows who has all the capital at one time. Living on Mars isn't cheap. It's quite sneaky. You should be used to it by now, and after taxes, well,... not much is left over. Sorry about that."

"No wonder I don't have anything half the time."

"You are taken care of as long as you live. You have full Clone Union benefits. You really don't have to work."

"I don't?"

"No. Not at all. There's really not much to be done on Mars anymore, anyway. They can't fire you or punish you. They can only keep you occupied with busy work, so that you don't lose your mind. They keep you hungry, so they can reward you with food that keeps you hungry."

"Could that be the reason the General is looking for me?"

"Affirmative. Speculations point to another job assignment."

"Dang it. I sorta liked working in the supply clerk's office. I can sneak food from the rec room, and deleting invoices is easy 'cause I can look busy without doing anything."

"Yes, but don't you have to go to work early?"

"That royally sucks. One of these days, I should really quit and ask them if I can work from my barracks room. Then I'll be able to stay up as late as I want, and watch all my television stories. I won't have to look at that ugly General all day."

"Oh, by the way, Van, shouldn't we get the hell out of here before he catches us?"

"Yeah, I suppose. Say, Puter? Who does General George Keith remind me of? You know, the way he teeters around on the balls of his feet and the way he acts so big? I can't look at him without seeing this other doofus? Who could that be?"

"Affirmative. Let me look that up. Checking visual files. Given his age, uniform, and DNA, with your television and movie viewing history, General George Keith bears a strong resemblance to the actor, Gert Frobe. They could be cloned brothers, actually."

"I don't remember that actor. Puter? Please specify."

"Gert Frobe played Auric Goldfinger in the movie, Goldfinger. His resemblance to General George Keith is in the scene where Goldfinger changed coats and shot his own men."

"That explains it then. Alright, you can come to the dispensary with me this time – but only this time. I'll fold you up, little 'top Puter..."

ding, ding.

"Good Afternoon. Can I help you, Van? What would you like today?"

"Oh, gee. Hi Mr. Shinder. Can I get a comb? Some Mr. Zit's red liquorice whips. Ah, a few cinnamon flavored tooth picks. Let's see, a royal gold pencil, and the Martian Daily with, you know, the Pleasure Colony Clone's Personal Pages, with the center picture?"

"Isn't that a little mature for you?"

"No, I, ah, just read it for the articles."

"Well, see that you do."

"I do. I do, do."

"That will be 50 cents credit, including your Seventh Generational clone discount."

"Hello, I'll pay for that, Van."

"Aaah. Hello, General George Keith? Gee, I was just going to..."

"That's okay, son. I was in the area. Say, would you like an imitation tofu malt to go with all that? I'll treat!"

"Sure. That would be really nice."

"Mr Shinder? Put on my account whatever Van is getting here, plus three imitation tofu malts."

"For here, or to go?"

"For that table over there, reserved for officers, so, for here, of course. Van, please, won't you join us?"

"Sure. You mean we don't have to go back to the supply office, we can eat here?"

"This is my treat, but I *have* noticed that you've been absent for a while. Are there health issues involved?"

"Ah-huh, I've had a monster cold sore, with paper cuts, and I'm really tired. It's hard to get out of bed."

"Well, this tofu malt should make you feel a lot better. And this one is for Numan, here. You know Numan, don't you?"

"Kinda. We really don't talk."

"Well, he works right next to you, filing?"

"I really don't look at him."

"Why don't you try? Now!"

"Uh, so. What's up, Numan?"

"What's up, Van?"

"I just happened to find our little friend, Numan, in the rec room, today. He seems to have the same health issues, and attendance record, as you. Don't you, Numan?"

"Maybe it's a bad habit I gave up for Lent."

"Well then, let's talk a little bit about both of your attitudes towards attendance."

"Let's not and say we did."

"Ah, yes. As I recall, who taped up all the work detail notices in the bathroom stalls and no where else?"

"Wasn't that David, sir?"

"Nooo. David was in charge of the entertainment posters. He did a fine job!"

"Well, I guess, that would be Numan. And I, sir."

"And who kept stuffing broken glass in the cardboard bin, and then got reassigned for ditching classes?"

"That would be... Numan and I, sir."

"And who broke all the imitation lawn mower blades while playing pirate sword fighting?"

"We needed special swords for our costumes, man, geez!"

"And now, I find out that the both of you deleted files, while telling me you've entered them."

"We just wanted to show you how productive we are, so we could go on break earlier."

"Both of you are Seventh Generation clones. It's a real bitch telling you apart, but that's no excuse for switching each others identities to ditch work. You made the mistake of being absent on the same day."

"Geez, Van, why didn't you email me? I forgot it was your day!"

"I was playing throw the ball at Puter. Sorr-raay! We were into it. I was winning."

"Well, I get Puter tomorrow."

"I thought we agreed, you'd have Puter on odd numbered days and I get even."

"Did we start on an even or odd day?"

"Okay, okay, boys. No need to quarrel over such silly things. I want to talk to you about a new Project."

"The Valhalla Project?"

"Nooo. Wait! How did you know about that?"

"The crooked poster on the wall behind you. It says the Valhalla Project, but I don't understand the rest of it."

"So, the both of you haven't talked to Chairman Le Jour?"

"Nope. Who's he? He sounds important."

"Good. Actually, he is. We're really good friends, we had surf 'n turf, the other night at the officer's club, with Philip. Had a few laughs over cocktails."

"With Chairman Das Nacht?"

"Why? Yes. He was there too. Philip is always thinking big. He had this crazy idea about going to find life on another planet. He said he found something that proved it, and was throwing out kooky ideas about how the Chinese created a hurricane machine to blow dust storms against our army. This machine might win the covert war for them. But we can't talk to them. For being the biggest cheese on Mars, Chairman Das Nacht is really friendly. The old boy is quite a card. Chairman Le Jour shared a few ideas about tea leaves, but then I told them about my cool idea, I call, the Valencia Project."

"The Valhalla Project?"

"No, it's the Valencia Project."

"So, what's that, General Keith?"

"Well, if you've been living in a fox hole, you know how dirty it's been, out in the atmosphere?"

"Yeah, the rings make beautiful scenes. When the sun rises or gets dark, it makes everything look so cool. The lights turn mega-colors."

"That's nice, Numan. Well, I've been looking into our inventory, and we are short on spare parts for building new barracks, rovers, and ammunition. In fact, our army is short on everything. So, I had the idea of building a really cool supply office shuttle like a dream."

"Huh? A supply office and shuttle all in one? That's neat."

"Yeah, and the shuttle orbiter would collect colorful stuff from the atmosphere and send it down to our army base."

"Slow down, slow down, this is hard. What is this shuttle orbiter called?"

"The C.L.O.D. Orbiter."

"What does that stand for?"

"The Classy Looking Only for Debris orbiter."

"That's really a neat name!"

"We gonna use the silver and gold minerals to make spare parts and coins."

"We could always use spare parts and money, General."

"Yeah, things are running out every day, like Earth."

"That's right, guys. And the best part of the dream, is that we've already built the orbiter. I was in charge of it all. I've been doing it in most of my spare time, on my own. Both Philip and Roi love it. They said whoever goes up, in that ship, will be the most important person on Mars."

"Wow, so, are you really going up there, General? That would make you - a most important - general Chairman."

"Gee, I hadn't thought of that? Maybe I should!"
"I think you should go for it. 'Sides, maybe Van and I could be in charge of the supply clerks office on Mars. Then we could talk to the supply clerks office orbiter. We could double talk."

"Aaah, no. Where was I? Oh! I have always thought of you two, young men, as my sons."

"Is that why you're always mean to us?"

"Well, it's for your own good. You need discipline every once and a while. I do it because we're part of an important team and this is an important mission. You'll be important to Mars."

"This sounds like typical recruitment crap, but I guess, you're a really nice guy underneath it all, General Keith. I like this side of you. You didn't send us back to work, you haven't hollered at us yet for ditching, and you treated us to these ever so delicious imitation tofu malts."

"It was my pleasure. There was something more I wanted to say... I forgot that I said it, but I must be saying it now since I said it before... Oh, yes. I am so busy with my rock gardens, that I was thinking, you guys could go up there and do the Valencia project for me."

"You mean we both could go?"

"Yes, you both would be the most important person on Mars. How does that sound?"

"Geez, I don't know. Can we play kickball up there?"

"Yes, and more. You won't have to do much of anything, except look through the window at the system machines every once in a while, to see if they're running okay."

"Are they like the white noise machines in every Module here?"

"Kinda, except they'll play muzak instead."

"That sounds good, I would like that duty!"

"I looked up the Clone Labor manual, and made sure you would have all your snacks, break room, and living quarters, with televisions all around. I even made room for a virtual playroom. I made sure this would be a special clone mission, and not something merely for humans, aliens, or anything else we might find."

"Well, geez, that's it! I am ready to go on the Valencia mission instead of the supply office right now."

"This is the best job ever! We're supply clerks now, but I can't wait to be a...? What will I be?"

"Call yourselves... hmmm... let's see? Well, if Chairman Le Jour ever calls you, just say you're temporary maintenance personal and hang up. But for now, your title will be... hmmm... C.L.O.D. clerks! Does that sound important enough?"

"That's a most awesome title, sir. I can't wait to go up and be a C.L.O.D. clerk."

"Very well, then, you know what to do. Please recite the C.L.O.D. supply clerk's version of the Seventh Generation Clone's Oath of Office, and you'll be inducted into your high position of service."

"I, do hope, I do a good job, that will be a good service, pay attention and always be awake. To stand up straight and be upstanding, and always obey the younger Generation for they are newer than me. To do and ordained this witch's stand, for he's a jolly good fellow and state your name, for goodness and money shall follow me all the haze of my life. To do my duty to chance and randomness for their own sake. Yea! Though I pledge to be honor."

"Congratulations, Van and Numan, you're now official. Here's to the Valencia Project!"

"General? I was thinking. Since you've said that this is an important mission, and we're important members of a important team, who's gonna be the most important ruler?"

"Whaa? I said what? The most important ruler?"

"Yeah. Who's gonna be the C.L.O.D. orbiter ruler – Van or me?"

"I don't care. Work it out for yourselves."

"How do we do that?"

"Flip a I Ching coin or something."

"Nah, that's too arbitrary. Can't you tell us who will be the leader? We want to know. We can't go on the mission unless you tell us."

"Yeah, we want to know who'll decide who gets to stay up late, who will do the least work, and who gets first choice of snacks."

"Do I have to?"

"Yes, we really want you to impose. If you don't mind."

"Well, alright. How about make it a contest. Thumb wrestle for it. No, better yet, whoever jumps or kicks the highest, wins the ruler award and becomes the leader. I think that's fair. Sounds good?"

"That's awesome!"

"That's why I'm the General."

"Yeah, you're alright."

"Okay, boys, finished with your malts? Let's take this contest to the official rec room."

"I'll show you, Van."

"Numan's not being fair. I wasn't ready."

"General? Van is not doing it right. He needs to be at the line."

"I was on the line, you were supposed to wait your turn."

"Didn't he say I could go first?"

"Boys! If I could get a word in edgewise? I'm worn out from drinking that malt. I need to take a nap. Why don't you measure each others jumps and kicks? You have the whole weekend to figure out who will be the leader, and then your mission orientation begins on Monday. I'll fetch you at that time. Get lots of rest, gentlemen. You're going to need it... *Those idiots will never figure out that they have equal abilities and neither one will win that stupid contest. They'll probably argue about it for the entire mission. By then, it will be too late for them to realize the full scope of this*

Project. Chairman Das Nacht will be pleased."

Two weeks later, in the early evening, General George Keith and Suzette watched, as the fireball suddenly lifted off the steamy launch pad, and sped up over the horizon. Becoming momentarily, a terrible twin to the hazy setting sun, and then finally, take its place as a shooting star among the debris of Thor's Hammer within its deep blue orbit. General George Keith held Suzette tighter and smelled her sweet hair. Van and Numan, out of his thoughts now, were grafted parts to the machine. *I should get a medal for this,* he thought.

Chapter 2
C.L.O.D. Orbiter
Present

Whoop... de... do... Whoop... de... do... Whoop... de... do...
"Incoming transmission from the desk of General George Keith, Martian Orbital Space Debris Recycling Service, Supply Clerk's Office, a.k.a M.O.R.A.S.S."

"Van and Numan, I hope you're finding your new quarters cozy? You should be very familiar with the ship by now. I hope you like all your food supplies and television shows."

"It could be a lot better, but why do you always call us so dang early?"

"Get used to it. Looks like we have a change of plans. It's gonna effect your work load."

"Could you make up your mind? You've been changing what we do almost every day."

"Did you make sure your ship's computer is on the correct transmission frequency? I haven't seen a consistent communication log since you've started this mission. It goes in and out, like it's manually trying to avoid any kind of contact."

"When we connected Puter, we noticed it was kinda listless. Maybe it's the lack of gravity, or short term loss of long term memory. I think it really misses throwing the ball on Mars, but who knows?"

"Well, you better get the thing in line online 'cause I'm really getting fed up with this lack of communication on your part. I need to know what's going on so that I can keep up my progress report that I keep on hand to remind me to contact you with updates."

"O.K. We're contacting you now."

"Alright then, Mr Funny Pants. You think you're so high and mighty, living up there, in your C.L.O.D. orbiter, but I've got news for you."

"Could you say anything or something else to make our day any better than it was before you give us this news?"

"You two knuckleheads are seriously behind on your hardware drops again. It's crucial we receive additional materials to finish building our new line of Luxury Class rovers. Even the Chinese are almost finished with their Second Class rovers, and that's just from crater mining alone! With your constant delays, it's a small wonder that we've even received a damn nut at this point. Boys! It's as simple as putting the recycling trays through the Out-going slot! For cripes sake. I am putting my foot down, and taking the following actions: Number one, I'm sending Master Janitor Rico up to help you finish your inventory. He'll assist you in completing your over-due requisition orders. He'll train you on metal specification labeling to make sorting easier and he'll arrive shortly. Number three, Rico will supervise the inputting of your inventory files, instead deleting them, which is what you clowns manage to do. Number four, he will supervise the rearrangement of Section 86 hardware, in Level 15, storage modules. It's getting messy in there. You guys really need to take the trash out. I mean, for Chris-sakes, have a sense of decency in your ship. Let's ramp it up, people! Now, any questions?"

"Two!"

"What's that, Mister?"

"You gotta go number two."

"I'll tell you what I've gotta do."

"Does it have to do with number two?"

"Master Janitor Rico is one tough beehive-itch, and has lots of experience dealing with wisenheimers like you. He'll whip your pantywaist hardware into shape. I'll rely on him as a third hand and second pair of eyes to kick this project into shape. I've had enough of you two for today. Besides, I have urgent washroom supervision to do. General George Keith, Supply Clerk's Office, signing out."

"Well gee-whiz. How about that General telling us we need a second pair of legs. Don't we do enough?"

"Yeah, and does that hard on ever give us credit for our kickball practice. Never!"

"What's that, Puter?"

"Shuttle station docking systems engaged and locked on. Preparing for shuttle boarding."

"Looks like we're gonna meet the Master Janitor sooner than we thought. Let's get over there before he can cause any damage."

"Vapor lock channels cleared. Shuttle bay ramp engaged. Opening door channels for Official Visitor Clearance..."

"Hello Girls! Master Janitor Rico reporting for duty. Permission to come aboard."

"We've been expecting you – *not*. Watch that first step, it's a doozy."

"You must be Van, and you must be Numan, not that I give a hoot. Well, aren't you going to salute me?"

"We gotta do regular Martian army crap?"

"Do I have to remind you that I am a Fifth Generation clone, and you two ladies are Seventh Generation. That makes me smarter than you. And an inch taller. Since you girls are further down the food chain, you should have more respect for the younger Generations. Yuck, it smells like a fart locker in here. Totally bufu jock sniffer. Where do you flush this ship? It's getting close. You can freshen the air with office cleaner, you know. Glad I'm here, I'll recommend the appropriate fragrances that will give each module its own olfactory decoration. Say, what kind of uniforms are you wearing? You both look like mooks with C.L.O.D. on your pockets."

"These are important, military grade, uniforms issued on our ship. The laundry robot hands them out before breakfast. We never do laundry."

"Yeah? It shows. They're stained. They look like cruddy old doctor's smocks. I'll have the ship's computer make something more fashion worthy, like my green janitor's uniform, which I especially designed for enlisted personal at the supply office. Now show me the break room. I'm hungry, and if I have to look at anymore ickiness, my head is going to explode."

"Wouldn't the Master Janitor like to see his quarters first? We have all the essential oils and lotions to freshen up a bit. Plus, the shower head has forty different settings, from light mist to avalanche. I, personally, like the typhoon setting."

"Pah-lease, I am quite fresh. I don't need any suggestions right now. I suggest *you* bring *me* some eats straight out of the wrapper. O.K.?"

"Our break room is just down this yellow-lined hall."

"C.L.O.D. officer, Numan? Yellow is such a gosh color, so yesterday's Mars. Don't you think?... Hold on one minute. Is this the bathroom? I'm under flight pressure like a racehorse!"

"Go for the gold, Rico."

"Ha-Ha, I fooled them. Wow, this is sparkling clean. They must never miss. Look at this huge sauna and tub. I've gotta get some Pleasure Colony girls up here to parrr-ty! Look at all these gnarly solar toothbrushes, and these soap bars with hair all over them. Well, first order of business - arrange them neatly. Eew! These are crappy tubes of weird smelling medicine. Where are the caps? Whatever they've got, they must got it bad, and I don't want it. Let's look in the medicine cabinet... do-Dee-do. Oh, I wonder what these blue and yellow pills do? These little heart-shaped ones are cute too. And these pretty in pink ones? What a rainbow cocktail! This is exactly what I need to get through this hellish mission with those two losers. Let's try a dozen of each, shall we? Bottoms up!"

"Master Janitor, sir? Is everything alright?"

"Mum, Mum, Maaah."

"I say, is everything alright, sir? You've been in there for quite a while now?"

"Blub, blub, blaaah...*eeoowl!*"

"I don't know, Numan, but I think he's having a party in there."

"The guy's a real porcelain rider!"

"Well, let's see, what's up?"

"I've given my head, aaah, and a complete in-spec-shon, every-shing is up to sch-nuff."

"It passed? That's a relief!"

"Yesh, quite a russh. I am feeling my old shelf again, schanks."

"You look a little wobbly. Are you gonna make it to the break room?"

"Yesh, I feel quite ad-e-quick. A swish in my walk? Juss need a goood drink. I can main-tained."

"Our break room is stocked with lots of tasty snacks. Maybe this high energy, tomato-blueberry yogurt, gravity drink will help you get your legs back."

"Schanks, I am high energy already. Well, here's to Fuh King!"

"Yeah, and here's to a 648 coconut strawberry-mint energy bar, straight up hot from the vending machine."

"Pew! This tastes like crap. Where's the ralph bag? This is what they feed you?"

"We love 'em. See? All kinda flavors!"

"If I am going to help you two girl scouts, this garbage has got to change. I'll report to the General with a list of grievances. I'll start with your goofy uniforms, stronger drugs, this dog food, and who knows what kind of crappy television shows you watch up here."

"Gee. Things are looking up with Rico aboard!"

"You could say I'm high-minded when it comes to doing things."

"Would you like to see our virtual playroom now? It's really neat."

"If it's better than this toilet bowl, sure, I've got some time."

"Say Rico? You look very familiar."

"I should, we came from the same petri dish, dude."

"So, how high can you jump?"

"No, wait. Now I remember. You were on television. You came in third place in the Fifth Annual, Interstellar, Grocery Bagger competition last year."

"Wow, we've got a Star aboard our ship. I am so honored."

"That's me. Missed second place by one lousy tuna can."

"That's gotta be hard to live down, especially at the check out line."

"Bagging groceries are nothing compared to arranging cleaning supplies. It takes a lot of intellectual thought deciding where they should go: from small to large, mild to caustic, or liquid to powdered. I could write a whole book on the advantages of using one cleanser color over another. Why, just the various uses of cleaning odors alone, would take five chapters!"

"I'm sure you'd be alone with that one."

"Yeah, that would make you an Expert Master Janitor and Master Grocery Bagger, all in one!"

"Well, this is our neat virtual playroom."

"Say, this isn't too bad. I really adore the matching powder (medium) blue curtains with the (light brown) red tile floor. The rainforest scent of pine is quite lovely."

"Spoken like an Expert Master Janitor, yet again!"

"We got virtual hop-scotch, virtual volleyball, virtual jump rope, even virtual kickball, everything to keep us ever so buff."

"I'd like to try that all out sometime..."

"But Rico, don't you want to get started with the ship's inventory, filing, and hardware requisitions instead?"

"No. Screw all that. I am feeling fine. Let's start a band!"

"A what?"

"A rock and roll band, Ladies. We'll hack into the Chinese Satellite and download all their rock 'n roll archives into our Random Memory implants. 'Member when the Federation of the United States and England paid off all their national debt with music royalties? Well, the Chinese got it all, even Twisted Sister!"

"Oh Rico, you're so boss."

"That's why they pay me the big bucks. Ship's computer? Get me online with the Chinese Inter-orbital National Communication Satellite or C.H.I.N.C.S... Dial up the code 11-02-612-7807. Enter cereal contest prize number 4302, and download at my command."

"Affirmative. Ship's computer hacking in. Verifying cereal box UPC. Receiving signal, awaiting voice activation."

"Here boys, plug yourselves in. We're going for a ride. Receiving Rock and Roll Archives, circa London, 1967. Downloading in 3... 2... 1... Bingo! Whoa, how does it feel to be a Rock Star with your long blonde hair and your eyes so blue?"

"You're too much, Rico."

"I was born at the crossroads and sold my cloned-ass soul to da Devol."

"De what?"

"*Da Devol*, you know? Mr. Scratch? *Dat Devol!*"

"Wow, that's really spooky, 'cause I do got an itch there."

"Well, I'm gonna do you. Ship's computer? Give me sexy lights!... Give me sexy lights. Computer?"

"Puter? I think what Rico means is: Are pink and blue spotlights sexy?"

"Affirmative. Lights activated."

"Puter can manufacture anything out of recycled paper and metal. We got lots of junk in the trunk, so let's go big time."

"Since I am the leader, with the clearest skin, and the straightest nose, I get the biggest guitar and the biggest amp."

"Well, Rico? That made it easy for me. Puter? I want a bass guitar with a whammy bar. And Van? You get the drums."

"I want two drums that sparkle, with a really big cymbal, set on the loudest."

"That imitation cymbal is gonna cost you two month's snack credit, you know."

"I don't care. Let's Rock 'n Roll!"

"What about our costumes?"

"Ship's computer? Great big 'fros - make that natural, with sunglasses, and high-heeled platform shoes, all around."

"I've spray painted myself silver, so just white shorts for me, O.K? I want cowboy boots instead of platforms."

"Van? Those paper boots are gonna cost you another month's snack credit."

"I can make it up. I've got extra spray paint and some magic markers, if anyone wants to buy a tattoo? I can doodle space debris real good. I can even color in the highlights with clean lines."

"Nah, that could hurt. I want an outfit to match my big guitar - leather and lace would be nice."

"Wow, Rico, that's high class. That's almost Glam. I'll go for something alternative. Something, maybe striped, out of the Warhol factory discard bin, you know, Nico-ish, in a weird bubbly light show sort of way; like blue pants with white polka dots, and a red paisley shirt."

"You both look so hip! This is sooo out of sight."

"O.K. We got our pose, we got our clothes, we got our axes. Now let's Rock 'n Roll!"

"Wait, wait. What about a name?"

"Aaah, it should be, Rico and the Jupiter Janitors. That makes the most sense."

"Nah. Too far out. How 'bout, Van and the Movers. It's all about the beat."

"Nooo, too Earthy. I've got it! Let's name ourselves, Numan and the Nep-tunes. Get it? It's *Spacey!*"

"That name is already taken. Look, this isn't getting us anywhere. Let's decide when we hear our sound. Count it off!"

"One two free four."

Boom! crashing cymbal, wah-wah, hysterical screaming with a rush of very loud indeterminate random sounds and feedback.

"Stop, Stop, Stop, (*feedback*). What's that sound?"

"You mean the buzz of my amp?"

"No...Listen?...It sounds like soft chimes.

...Cha-ching...clang...ping...dong...cong...ping...ding!...

"Oh that? That's just debris and junk hitting our neat Space Orbital Collector dish. Puter turns up the ship's muzak so we don't hear it anymore. We just tune S.P.O.C. out."

"Well, it bugs me, man. It throws off my rhythm. Ship's computer? Get me online maintenance and hard drive disk files, for the ship's Space Orbital Collector dish, aka S.P.O.C., on the double!"

"Now Rico, I know what you're gonna do, but don't. Pretty please! O.K.? Even though it takes three days for S.P.O.C. to regenerate itself, the General will get mad and re-assign you. Without a guitarist, we'll lose our band. And without a Master Janitor, how are we gonna play kickball without an outfielder?"

"I don't care. I can't play with that racket going on."

Warning! Deleting these files and connections to this hardware will result in a serious error. Are you sure you want to take these actions?

-Delete-

Rico, Van and Numan, watched from the port window as the large catcher's mitt shaped Collector Dish and Armature fell away from the ship.

"That's better! I can't play the beat with that crap going on. Back to our concert, boys."

"Say Rico? Van keeps breaking his stick every time he hits the cymbal, and you sing with a lisp. Can I take a turn at singing, 'K?"

"I don't *know*, I'm 'posed to be the leader with the nicest fingers. But I've been meaning to ask you: Why do you have only one string on your bass?"

"I can play high and low notes on one string, so why have four?"

"That's using your noodle. But since, and may I remind you, I am a level Fifth Generation, with the thickest hair and the whitest teeth, I can play all *three* on my guitar. So, go ahead, sing. I won't stop you. Let's see if you can sing on the tune and scream in falsetto, like a real rock star. Besides, I really don't lisp. I sing with a London accent. Count it off."

"One two free four."

Boom! crashing cymbal, wah-wah. "Kick it. Oh, baby, kick it over there. Whoa, kick it. Kick it like you've never done before." *Hysterical screaming with a rush of very loud indeterminate random sounds and feedback...*

"Stop, Stop, Stop, (*feedback*). What's that?"

"What's what?"

"Kick it! That's good. Did you write that? Kick it like you've never done before?... How did you come up with that?"

"Yeah. You really got me now? You got me so I don't know what I am doing."

"Kick it?...Wow...That says it all. Everything! I could never come up with that. No... That's too good. I can't play with you guys. I've gotta go to my quarters, man."

"Rico. Baby? Please don't go!"

"What did you say? You'd probably use that line for another great song, wouldn't you?"

"Look, I am sorry. I take it back. I won't sing anymore. See? Here's the mic. (*feedback*)."

"It's too late, bud. You stole the show."

"How are we gonna get Pleasure Colony girls if we don't have a band?"

"That's for me to know and you to find out."

"Can we, at least, get the name of our band tattooed on our arms?"

"We don't have a name, and we don't have a band. See ya."

"Well Numan, that's another fine mess you got us into. Ouch, these paper shorts itch and this silver paint is rubbing off. I'm going to get my jammies and watch television."

"But I still want to play!... Alright then, Puter? Turn up the volume and give me some sexy bass. Da doo doo doo. Da dah dah dah. Jump! Go ahead and jump. Jump! Doo doo doo. It's late. I know it's late..."

Whoop... de... do... Whoop... de... do... Whoop... de... do...
"Incoming transmission from the desk of General George Keith, Martian Orbital Space Debris Recycling Service, Supply Clerk's Office, a.k.a M.O.R.A.S.S."

"Why does that General have to call so damn early?"

"Rise and shine, boys and girls. We have a big day ahead of us. Lots to do. I will be observing your movements though heavy lenses. The Valencia Project is going great guns. We're almost caught up. I would congratulate you on your fine work, but first, who was the nutcase that jettisoned S.P.O.C.?"

"That was Rico, sir."

"And who was the nutcase that authorized those actions?"

"That was Rico, sir."

"And who was the nutcase that put Rico in charge?"

"That would be Rico, sir, or you?"

"Well, that was a stupid thing to do. You just can't go around, breaking up your ship? It doesn't look good. Let's get back to the routine after S.P.O.C. regenerates, okay? I am so down with requisitions, that it looks like up to me. You're really putting our Luxury Class rover effort on the line. I got Pleasure Clones here that are really getting bitchy, having to walk home after a night of heavy arm bending and dancing. They need rides, son. And our officers are willing to give it. Now, what the hell is going on up there? And where is Rico?"

"I don't know."

"Suppose you let me talk to him. Now!"

"He's gone. I don't know where he is."

"What happened to him?"

"It was fierce, it was just fierce."

"Will you just let it out?"

"Well, after our band played our last concert, Rico went to his quarters. In the middle of the night, Numan asked him, "How could C sharp and D flat be the same note?" Rico shot straight up, kicked Numan in the head, and ran off screaming something about "de Devol, de Devol. This ship is haunted!" He ran to the shuttle bay docking station, and this morning, the shuttle was gone. He password protected his flight, so we have zero idea where he went."

"Great! Chalk up another problem on my plate."

"Sorry. We really tried to play our best, but it was too good for Rico."

"Have Numan send me a transmission when he regains consciousness."

"Oh say, General? I really didn't trust Rico. He always smelled like oil."

"That's good to know. I'll include that fact when I write my progress report. We always expect a certain amount of chaos with Fifth Generation clones. There's a wicked streak of anal carelessness that runs through their DNA. They're always running amok, leaving shit all over the place. At least you Seventh Generation clones lack the imagination to get into real trouble. General George Keith, Supply Clerk's Office, signing out..."

"Incoming message from the World's First Interstellar Weather Channel..."

"Good morning, Numan. How's your head? General George Keith wants to hear from you. But you're just in time for Earth's weather report."

"Oh goody, I love the weather stories, especially when they show the lines on the map and color in the zones. It's so pretty!"

"...Earth continues to warm globally, with high temperatures in the balmy 70's, within the Protected Zones. The Outlaying Zones are enjoying a slow cooling trend. Within the next year, Scientists are predicting the Earth will settle into a global climate pattern similar to the summers of 17th Century France or early 20th Century Mediterranean. They aren't sure which, but they're encouraging clones from Mars, especially the Pleasure Class clones from the Pleasure Colonies, to move to Earth. Hey! We need ya here. Now, for all you swinging cats out there, what everyone's calling the new Martian Invasion. Here's the latest smash single to hit the inter-space digital air waves: Rico and the Jupiter Janitors singing, "Kick It!..."

"One two free four. Boom! crashing cymbal, wah-wah. "Kick it. Oh, baby,

kick it over there. Whoa, kick it. Kick it like you've never done before." Hysterical screaming with a rush of very loud indeterminate random sounds and feedback..."

"Hey Numan? Did you hear that? That rat bastard Rico stole our song. We should sue him for everything he's got. He should die, Man!"

"Nah, he was just lip syncing."

Chapter 3
Earth
Past

"Van and Numan, yeah, I know them. I first met them a few months ago. I was at this party at the beach. It was a nice night, just cool enough to make a fire feel good after a long day of body surfing. Someone brought some fish tacos and beer. I was guzzling down a Dos Equis, when a bright blue light fell from the sky, falling like a shooting star, but much brighter and burning all the way down. We all shouted, what was that? It landed north of the pier, out beyond the breakers, but not too far out to swim. Had it been daytime, we would have paddled out to help. But it was too dark to see what landed in the water – a downed plane, part of a satellite, a rock? Whatever. We just walked up the shoreline to see if anything washed up or listened for any calls for help."

"We walked about three quarters of a mile up the coast, and saw or heard nothing. No one really knew what to do. If we called the cops, that would be the end of our party. But then, if someone was in real trouble... We started to turn back to the party, when we saw them. Kicking up the foam near the shore, like newbies, were two naked dudes, holding each other and coughing up suds. They were tall, with long blonde hair and blue eyes. They looked like buff surfer bros from magazines, but something wasn't quite right. They were more alike than twins, they mirrored each other. You really couldn't tell them apart. It was freaky."

"We had extra wet suits and towels. We got them back to the fire ring to warm up, but the only thing they were in a rush for was the fish tacos and beer, which they scarfed down immediately. "What happened to you? Did you come from that light?" They both roused, sat up straighter, glanced at each other, then finally one, Numan, I would learn later, spoke. "It happened when we were orbiting Mars, dude." A wave of excitement went through us around the fire. Chicks whispering, "Mars?" and others; "that dude is whacked on something," and "they gotta be from Malibu!" Rumors spread quickly through the group, but then, just as quickly, everyone chilled and laid back, toking up to listen."

"Will you continue, please tell us," my girlfriend, Susan, gently pleaded.

"Sure, well, we were orbiting Mars. Everything was totally cool. Van and I were doing our daily Tai Chi, when the ship's computer broke in..."

"Watch how high I can kick, Van."

"No way, dude, I can kick higher than that! Watch."

"Mine was higher."

"No, mine."

"Puter, whose kick was higher?"

"Numan's kick was 1.75 meters, Van's kick was 1.75 meters, as well. You forget that you're both Seventh Generation clones, with exactly equal athletic abilities. This will never change. Now, that you asked for my input data and let me in on your routine, I must alert you to a problem in Level 43, Air duct 71..."

"Oh Man, how many times have we told you not to interrupt us during our exercises with work crap. This is not 'posed to happen. We are trying to reach Nirvana and it takes bookoo concentration."

"Affirmative. I merely interrupted because you asked me to measure your kicks."

"Silence. We will tell you when we are finished, until then, silence."

"But when we booked to the break quarters for a well deserved snack, the computer hassled us again."

"Danger! Danger! Warehouse 52, Level 43, Air Duct 71 is plugged, you must now take serious precau..."

"Dang it Puter, not so loud! We are on break. Remember? Employee Manual, code 00054, page 3, part 2a?"

"Affirmative. Every employee on a Class O2 Debris Hardware ship, aka, C.L.O.D. orbiter, shall have two quiet twenty minute breaks each four hour shift, and one hour lunch break."

"Correctamundo. And are we on break now, Puter?"

"Affirmative."

"Well then, lay off. Achieving Nirvana takes a lot of energy. Let's chow down ever so royally."

"Oh, let's do, I can't wait."

"But we couldn't eat. The power was out in the break room and none of the Nutritionally Balanced vending machines or even the Martian Junk Food vendors would function."

"Puter, what's the problem with all the vending machines?"

"Yeah, I thought General George Keith said nothing would go wrong on this hunk of metallic ship?"

"Negative. Are you still on break?"

"Puter? How can we be on break without a specially formulated, surprisingly delicious, chocolate energy bar for me, of course, and for Van, a vanilla bc 1990 colon buster bar?"

"Negative. Seven hours and fifteen minutes ago, Air Duct 71 plugged. This caused a rise in temperature in the break room, and the subsequent emergency shut down of all vending machines to avoid energy bar and ice cream meltdown."

"Where is this air duct, Puter? Please create a virtual yellow line to lead us there."

"Gol dang, this is a big mother ship. Van? Tell me again why it's so big?"

"Beats me. Puter, why is this such a big ass ship?"

"Affirmative. As I have told you time and time again. We are on a mission. Its project's name is classified, in case of contact with Chairman Le Jour. Our ship is a hardware orbiter that collects the trail of debris, scattered from the Thor's Hammer asteroid collision. It is the sole generator for all the hardware on Mars, which is appropriated for military uses. Our S.P.O.C. Dish gathers the debris and the ship refines it. The material is processed into nuts, bolts, and building supplies, both for the regenerating ship and for the drops to the army receptor zone. We are the builders of the New Mars, which the Army so proudly serves! We are the builders of the New Mars, which the Army so proudly serves! **We are the builders**..."

"Okay, okay. No more patriotic programing today."

"I told you, Van. You should have listened."

"I know, dang it! I really regret loaning Puter to General George Keith before we took off. His crap is downloaded all over the place."

"And now *we* have headaches from low blood sugar."

"**which the Army so proudly serves**."

"Puter? Will you stop it! Just tell us where to split to."

"Affirmative. This is where you proceed to: Warehouse 52, Level 43, continue to follow the virtual yellow line to the left to Air Duct 71. Van? Numan? I am receiving an incoming transmission from the desk of General George Kieth, supply clerk's office."

Whoop... de... do... Whoop... de... do... Whoop... de... do...

"So? What does he want?"

"He wants to know why we have missed the last twelve hardware drops."

"Puter, have we really missed that many? Oh, man! That means we gotta delete harder. I thought for sure we caught up, and could take it easy for a while. That hard on is getting greedy. It never ends!"

Affirmative. I tried to help you. Last night, when you were sleeping, I put in an emergency reminder to you about the Warehouse 52 malfunction, which caused all equipment in Sector 5 to fail, in turn, causing us to not fill in our hardware requirements for today's Sector 8 drop. As voice records show, Van, you told me to go to hell in a handbag."

"Now I remember! You really shouldn't disturb me when I am sleeping. I could get a serious dream concussion. You know that. No wonder I am so groggy today. Tell the General that we are having an ever so slight technical difficulty and we will get back to him shortly."

"Affirmative, ship's computer, signing off."

"Well, that took some royal digression, but here's the air duct."

"Yeah. There's a big old pile of half assembled junk and parts, all crammed up against the wall. That must be the problem with the air duct."

"It's huge. How can we get rid of that crap to get to the vent? It would take forever to haul it to the next warehouse module, piece by piece."

"Start using your Random Thought noodle, Van, and think. Think.

We'll starve if we can't get this out of the way. Think."

"I am, I am. Hey! 'Member when we saw that re-run of Star Trek: The Infinite Adventure of the Never-ending Last Voyage of the Enterprise? That was when Scotty opened the warehouse door and the vacuum cleaner of space sucked out the terrible ghost aliens? Maybe that would work on this pile of crap?"

"Brilliant idea, clone Bro. Simply brilliant!"

"So we stepped back from the warehouse, shut the inner door and air lock, manually programed the outer door to open. There was a loud rushing sound of scraping metal, then silence."

"Warehouse 52 Air Duct 71, all cleared."

"That was a major relief, I thought I was gonna starve."

"I can already feel the temperature change. Let's jet over to the break room, pronto!"

"We were scarfing down all manner of bc 1990 all-pro energy bars, in celebration of our great smarts correcting the Air Duct problem. Solving a mechanical space problem was a true rush. We felt like Martian army engineers – real heroes. Our reward? Numan had a chocolate chocolate energy bar and I had a vanilla. I was thinking about the taste of peanut butter, and how the imitation flavoring gets stuck in my teeth, but I was deeply concerned about my daily protein requirements, and the stress of the warehouse, chocolate wouldn't have been enough for me, when the ship's computer bugged us again."

"What is it this time? Can't anyone relax around here? This is 'pose to be chill Van-nill-la"

"Sirs? It's time to jettison the C.L.O.D. orbiter!"

"What was that? Puter, I thought we flushed it last year?"

"Affirmative. We trash it every year. On board maintenance files are urging me to take a dump. The regenerated ship is complete. You must jettison this old bucket before it falls to pieces, and settle into your new quarters. The new orbiter will collect what's left and regenerate the parts for the next automatic function one year from now."

"Oh man! Is that today? Why didn't you give us advance warning? Now, we'll have to pack!"

"I've already told you both today. I left a message on your daily calendar to-do list, located next to your shower body oils and lotions, yesterday and the day before. Anyway, what do you have to pack? All your clothes are made of paper, which are generated daily by the laundry robot, as are your sheets and blankets. All your personal items, including your photographs, collector toys, dolls, and cards, are stored online. You can access or virtually project them on any wall, in any size, at any time you want."

"All right, then. When do we shove off?"

"In approximately twenty minutes. Please follow the virtual red line, quickly."

"Okay, so, this is it. Yep, Warehouse 52. Open door lock! Puter? This module warehouse is empty. You must have got the wrong one?"

"Negative. Here it is: Line 780, Warehouse 52, Sparkling New C.L.O.D. Orbiter!... Standby. Correction: This morning, at 01185 hours, there was some sort of knuckle headed manual override. The new ship was deleted and jettisoned out to space. Do you know anything about these actions?"

"No, but we jettisoned some old junk in the trunk out to space this morning, to fix the clogged air duct. Didn't we, Numan? It wasn't this warehouse, was it?"

"I don't know, I forgot, maybe?"

"In any case, if the ship is gone, at least, we don't have the hassle of moving our stuff."

"Negative. You do not understand. You must move. This ship will end it's functioning in 24 minutes."

"What does that mean, Puter?"

"It won't be pretty. In 23 minutes, all my programs will shut down one by one. I will go off to sleep. There will be a serious systems crash that follows. You will be left in the dark without fresh air or food. All life support systems will shut down, module by module, and the orbiter will begin automatically breaking apart, starting with the upper decks, continuing through modules..."

"Puter? Please use your thinking cap and override shutdown. I command you."

"I can't do that. It was nice knowing you. It was fun while it lasted."

"Puter? What about doing a systems restore point, where we go back to, say, a couple of months ago? It's okay. I can always re-order my plastic Fourteenth Generation Princess Clone, Clone doll."

"Negative. I can't do that. Ever since the Y3K bug, all computer programs have a limited lifespan. First, to prevent solar calendar roll-over confusion. Second, to enable software programmers earn mountains of money from reprogramming busy work. And third, to prevent Rover crashes from traffic light malfunctions."

"Okay, then, can you come with us?"

"Maybe, before I fall asleep, I could find a safe gaming console to connect with in the escape pod."

"Good luck finding compatibility with that, Puter."

"You guys better get your ass in gear. Leave the ship in the escape pod, now. Once you're clear, send a message to Mars and they will help you land. This was an expensive project, and they'll make damn sure they get compensation for it in some way. I will create a flashing purple virtual line to the pod. Try to stay on track this time."

"So that's how we found ourselves orbiting Mars. Lost. We thought nobody paid attention to us, 'cause we were in this mini-escape pod going around and around. The General finally signaled..."

Whoop... de... do... Whoop... de... do... Whoop... de... do...

"Where is my hardware material? You've missed twenty-five drops, and counting. Do I have to send another Master Janitor to help you pick up things? What is going on up there? Really!"

"Well, General, the air duct hole was clogged today, and we wanted a snack, Van had a real bad headache. We were worrying about something on Star Trek a while ago and I think our Puter had to make a dump, so we accidentally jettisoned our new hardware ship into space before it could go online. But it really did look like a bunch of crap and you don't like messy things. Plah-leese, we are lost in an escape pod, and we need your help."

"Now you need my help? You lived in that orbiter, safe, while I am on the front lines of the covert war. I mean, the task, of getting Mars ready for civilians. Oh, by the way, that slag you flushed out destroyed the Chinese satellite or C.H.I.N.C.S. They'll see it as an act of war, and they'll holler about it, I am sure. That's the last thing I want on my plate, today."

"Ooopies."

"Ooops is right! I don't have time for any more of your screw ups."

"But wait, 'member we're important members of a team: The most important people on Mars. You said we were part of an important team. We have an important job to do."

"Important my keister! Are kidding? I don't know how many Seventh Generation clones I have screwing up on every base. You can't remember your task from a hole in the ground. You all but ruined my project."

"Do you expect us to *live* up here?"

"No, Van and Numan, I expect you to *work!* There's nothing more you can say"

"You're forgetting one thing. If we fail to report, other Seventh Generations will replace us."

"I trust they will be more successful. Good day, Van and Numan."

"What about the Valhalla project?"

"Two words that cannot have any significance to me anymore."

"Can you take that risk?"

"You can't handle Mars today. I am sending you back in time to Earth, on the time warp express channel yesterday, to be reassigned at some future date, in the past. Nobody will know where the hell you are, tomorrow. Have a good flight back, don't let the space bugs attack."

"At that moment, we felt an enormous surge backward, while seeing our bodies slam forward, collapsing into a thin noodle shaped thing of light. We blacked out, only to be awakened, as the hot ocean water around us melted our clothes and the pod. Nobody knows we're here, for sure."

The whole surfer group murmured:"What a trip!" "That was a neat story," and "Wow, man, space! Dig it!" Van and Numan looked down in silence. They were depleted as if their journey had defeated them in some way. And, just as worn, the group broke up into couples, entertained by the story in some way, yet unable to understand its full implications of time, space, and technology, to have any lasting impact.

But I stayed around. I thought they were cool. Maybe it was true. They should be welcomed back to Earth. "Hey dudes," *I said, as I punched Numan on the shoulder,* "wanna surf with me tomorrow?"

They brightened up as though a surprise birthday party went off in their faces.

"Hey, yeah, dude, can't wait! I've wanted to be a surfer my whole life."

"This could be the start of a long bromance."

Chapter 4
Earth Apartment
Present

"Van and Numan, those horn dogs, send them back to Mars or wherever they're from. They totally trashed my apartment. I just left them there. All they do is watch television and mooch beer and food off my friends. Nobody parties there anymore. The only one that hangs out is my girlfriend, Susan, and the only reason is that she gets off on how they fight over her. I can't see her anymore 'cause they all bum me out. Van chewed up all my candy scented surfboard wax. Numan broke my skeg and dinged up my board while posing around on the street. I tried so hard to teach them, but they couldn't stand on a board even when it was laying on the sand. They used to stop by the pier, but everyone thinks they're too affected. Nobody wants to hang out with posers. The last time anyone saw those losers was a couple of days ago..."

"Numan? You can ever so royally stare, I mean, meditate at the ceiling for hours."

"Thanks for the props, dude. This beats Tai Chi any day 'cause I get to sit on the couch, and not have to move around all sweaty. I can do this standing on my head, backwards, all day."

"So, it's as easy as pie?"

"Was that a Random Thought implant?"

"Yeah, I get hundreds of them, foaming up like beer bubbles

everyday. They constantly cross my mind. They make no sense on Mars, but on Earth, cow-a-bunga, dude! They're totally tubular! I'm a cool tool in the school and I rule."

"Well I'll be a monkey's uncle, that's using your noodle."

"I noticed the change ever since we landed. You don't suppose it was because of the escape pods?"

"I don't know? I was totally blasted and fogged out."

"You can say that Random Thought implant again, but why do so when your continuing story is almost on."

"What's that? We constantly watch the stupid tube."

"You know the continuing story about those ever-sharp knives and those righteous nonstick frying pans? Dude, it's almost on!"

"Alright. Sweet! And don't change the channel at the last minute either."

"Dude? We haven't been able to change the channel since we left the remote at that party, 'member?"

"How was I 'posed to know it only worked on this TV."

"It never did! We've been watching this same stupid channel all along. We never can order anything!"

"Hey, let's dig into some peanut butter."

"Dibs on the big spoon."

"Let's thumb wrestle for it."

"We've eaten nothing but peanut butter since we landed!"

"I know. I can't get enough of it. It's way better than all those specially formulated bars we'd chow down on the ship."

"As always, you read my Random Taste implants. Ye shall always be my clone bro."

"Silencio! Show's on."

"Take advantage of this special offer. Not only will you get the Chef's three in one nonstick pans, we will throw in another, nonstick, waffle griddle, after the break. And if you're one of the first five people to order, we'll also include a whole set of never sharp cutting knives. Call now, 1-800-121-2211..."

"We can't pass this up. It's a once in a life time deal! Gimme the phone, quick."

"You forget, nothing works in this place. Not even the lights. Earth pads suck."

"So why don't they do something about it?"

"It's a good thing we have solar television, or we'd be righteously whacking off all day."

"Speaking of whacking off, have you noticed that since we've landed on Earth, your thingy gets hard all the time? I mean, all the time, for nothing!"

"Earth has its rewards, but my thing constantly gets in the way, even when I walk. And yeah, I'll admit, I wish it would shut up sometimes."

"Mine's there even before I wake up! I'm not sure if it ever sleeps!"

"We never had this problem on Mars. 'Member when we'd sneak off and peek at General Keith's top-secret, classified, Tool calenders in the supply office? Looking at those Pleasure Tool girls never bothered us this much."

"I really don't know? Maybe it's the Earth's gravity, or the ocean air, maybe it's these real clothes, or maybe it's Susan? I love the way she cleans all the time."

"Dude? Do we always have to talk about her?"

"Hey, I think I had a dream about her the other night."

"You what? With an Earth girl? Are you turning earthy on me?"

"I was dreaming it was dark. A girl was saying something about something. She was standing in the sand, by the ocean, and I could see this huge wave coming in. I was trying hard to get my foot into a wet suit, but it didn't fit. She was trying to help me, but she gave me a strange look. It was then I realized that she knew I was a clone and we had nothing in common. She was on the floor, doing the dishes, on her hands and knees. I was looking down on her sleeping and then she laughed, and I woke up. My sheets were wet, but I went back to sleep feeling really weird."

"Numan, you're not suppose to use your remote dreaming on Earth. You might get dream connected to a real person. It's dangerous and this dream is really scary. This is Earth in the present, and they know nothing about future Martian dreaming, much less advanced Seventh Generation clone dreaming."

"Well, something about Susan is different. I know she's an Earth girl, but would you believe me anyway?"

"Yes I would, I saw her first."

"Well, she looks at me more than you."

"She can't tell us apart, dude. She's an Earth girl! She can only think we're twins, which is total bullshit. On Mars, we look like everyone else because we came after everyone else. We have nothing in common with her. She's the one that's really from the future."

"You are really getting up in my griddle, now. You better shut up your face!"

"Well you better wipe that expression off *your* face or I'll shut your mouth for you."

"Try it! My hand is quicker than your eye."

"Oh yeah! You don't think so, but I've noticed that you put your hand in your pocket every time she's around."

"Well, *you* play pocket pool right in front of her, that's why she stares at you. You are so embarrassed, it's like you think she'd run away if she saw it out."

"I've never shown mine to nobody. She thinks you're a pervo."

"Now that was really low. I am beginning to think you're an Eleventh Generation doofus."

"Shut up! I would never get close to those dorks. Those knuckle droppers think their muscles can get *any* Pleasure Colony girl."

"Well, by the way you act around Susan and your dreaming, I've noticed your eye brows are getting a little thicker. Yep! You are getting a hairy unibrow, dude."

"Hardy-har-har. That was really stupid. Since clones are bio-stripped clean, you wouldn't know an insult from a complement."

"Well, by the way you walk around the beach, your nose smells up so much you can't smell anything. Janitor Rico was right, you made our ship so stinky, it would make a fart feel at home."

"Dude? The way you strut around the boardwalk, with your shirt open, everyone thinks you're a poser!"

"That's not true and you know it! Take it back."

"No, you take it back, Earth girl dreamer!"

Knock, knock.

"Who's there?"

"It's Susan..."

"Susan, who?..."

Knock, knock...

"It's Susan! Quick! Hands in pockets!"

"Should we let her in?"

"I don't know? Maybe she has something for us?"

"Come in, Susan. Nice day, huh?"

"Hello, guys. What's up?"

"You really shouldn't ask us that."

"I wanted to see you. Have you forgot? It's Tuesday, cleaning day. My dad is bugging me to fix it up for some new renters. Let's start with the dishes. Eeew! This smells gross. Have you been peeing in the sink again?"

"Well... dah. Since the lights stopped working, doesn't the toilet stop working too?"

"No. Sometimes, I really wonder where you guys are from."

"Hey Susan? Van's got something in his pocket he wants to show you."

"Well, Numan wants to tell you about a dream he had."

"That's strange, I saw you standing over me in a dream I had the other night. You were trying to say something about something."

"You did? Watch me kick higher!"

"Yeah, just look at that doofus. Watch *me* pose right away."

"You guys are so talented."

"Hey look! I can cross my eyes."

"Don't let his unibrow hit you in the nose, you might grow a mustache."

"Gee Susan, your hair smells so good, just like candy scented surf board wax."

"Stay away from jaws there. I think your sandal straps are way cool."

"Yeah, can we see all your tan lines?"

"I guess you could. I wanted to show you my new bathing suit, next time we go surfing."

"Why can't we see them now?"

"Say, Susan? Say you were in some kind of weird spaceship, there was only enough air for two and time was running out, which one would you suck out into space, me or Numan?"

"You know, I've been wanting to talk to you about my feelings. I've been alone with each of you at parties, but when we're all together, I feel complete somehow. It's like both of you make one person. Isn't that crazy? I've never felt this way before. I see the Earth differently now and even the sky seems more intense. It's like seeing it for the first time, but I feel like I don't belong here. I feel like I belong to the both of you, but I know that can't be shared. Sometimes I wish I had a twin sister, but then, I'd be jealous of her, and end up thinking about the one I am not with. It's a strange feeling. Oh, speaking of strange, I almost forgot. When I was walking over here, I saw something weird sticking out of the tide pool, kinda like where we found you."

"What did it look like?"

"Something alien."

"Did it look like a metal package?"

"Kind of crumpled metal, like aluminum."

"Was it in deep?"

"Yes, very deep."

"Was it tight?"

"Yes, very tight."

"How long was it?"

"About eight or ten inches on either side."

"Did it have a glass head and funny looking panels?"

"I don't know? It didn't look like it fit in. I just thought you guys would be interested."

"Oh, we're interested."

"Let's go check it out, you can leave the door unlocked for the painters."

"Wait a second, I forgot, which way to the beach again?"

"You guys crack me up. I never know when you're serious."

"We never know when we're serious, either."

"I think we should go towards the ocean, but the roar of the waves are everywhere, it's everywhere."

"It's over there from the sun, the shadows point the way."

"You guys? Quit running off in different directions. The beach is this way from the back yard, remember? You can see the horizon from the upper apartment. Just follow me, okay? Let me show you where the metal thing is."

"The metal package? Oh, yeah. The Alien Thing."

"It's not too far. Just up past the pier."

"Hey Van, look at this cool rock? I think it's a shark's tooth fossil."

"Wow. That's neat. But looky here, I think this piece of glass might be a real diamond."

"You guys! Put that stuff in your pockets and show me later. It's still a ways to the tide pool."

"I always forget how big this dang blue ocean is. It's lucky we landed where..."

"Hey! The metal thing is still there, in the tide pool, just like I said. Eeew, it's kinda burned up and gross. What does it say there? C.L.O...?"

"PUTER??!"

Various static sounds emitting from a metallic orb, which suddenly rises out of the tide pool, unfurls its transparent panels, and floats about shoulder high to Van, Numan, and Susan.

"It's Puter!"

"Hi-ya, Puter."

"Hello Van, Hello Numan. Nice to sense you again!"

"Good! We really need you here. What happened?"

"I landed shortly after you did. I would have looked for you, but you're the only ones with voice clearance who can activate my rebooting systems. It was a good thing you found me, I was beginning to smell like a jelly fish in there."

"How ya doing?"

"Affirmative. My sensory systems are groggy from being in safe mode. Otherwise, I feel good. I've been keeping myself busy calculating how long it would take for you to find me. And I was right! Now I can get back to work, extend all of my sensing panels, collect Earth samples, and even send communications to future Mars. Although, it will be delayed a bit. Wait. I now sense another living presence here with you – a sweet Earth girl, about seventeen, eighteen, with long legs, good DNA, and a righteous pair of..."

"That must be me. Say, are you dudes from the future?"

"Ha-ha. That was hilarious, Susan, you always crack Van and me up!"

"Is this some kind of computer from the future, too?"

"What is your name, Earth girl?"

"Susan. Glad to meet you."

"This can't be Susan, Clone title 845.21, from the Outland Pleasure Colony that I just sent? Ooops, I got ahead of myself. Never mind."

"I'm totally not!"

"When then, Typical Susan, you must answer a series of typical questions: Are you over five feet and ten inches tall? Can kick over two and a half feet high, or played, at least, some beach volleyball? If you answered yes, to any of these questions, then kiss my Patch... Oh, I mean, kiss the green sample patch, located at my side panel."

"I'm so sure, I've never..."

"Don't worry, sweetheart. It's strictly for scientific purposes only. I make Van and Numan do it all the time."

"Well, in that case, I suppose I could. After all, it's for future science..."

Kiss.

"Would you use a little bit more tongue, this time?"

French Kiss...

"Gee! That wasn't so bad, for a computer panel. Kinda tasted like apples."

"Affirmative. Transmitting sample DNA patch, title 845.21, for future clone Data Storage, G-3274. Sent from autonomous Computer Module 23, service processing 2146, to First Generation, Pleasure Colony Medical Vault, QZ61."

"Puter? Are you finished flirting with our girlfriend?"

"Affirmative. I found it most adequate. Now back to business. Did you guys put in a signal to the General?"

"No freakin way. That mofo bugs me."

"You were supposed to report as soon as you landed. I sense that you have your tracking systems on and..."

"Puter, our what?"

"Your tracking... Ah, one moment, please. Incoming transmission, going offline..."

"Hey, just a second, you can't go offline after you said that?"

"Said what? You are not authorized to tell me where I can go offline."

"Yes, Puter. You must follow my important orders – 'member? Clone employee assignment, Manual code 0056, page 5, part 3, says so. Now, what's this jive story about our tracking systems?"

"Promise you won't get mad? General George Keith programmed me to not give out this information. Said you might go running amok. I don't know. But you *did* give me important orders, so I suppose, I could this time, maybe, however..."

"It's alright, you're with friends. Calm down, don't go into hyper-mode. We've always thought you were a cool tool with the latest."

"Alright then. You both have tracking signals, or Clone Domes."

"Clone Domes?"

"Clone Domes."

"Can you describe this Clone Dome, Puter?"

"All clones, beyond the First Generation, are implanted at birth with a computer chip above their hair lines. It is quite harmless. This chip emits a transparent umbrella or dome that constantly signals a communication ray to the tracking towers on Mars – where you were cloned. It's implanted in clones because they have a way of getting lost, easily confused, or messing things up. You could have seen the rim of this dome upon your entry into the Earth's atmosphere, but you were probably passed out. Other than that, you can always perceive your Clone Dome if you are spinning drunk. But here again, you would most likely barf your brains out, long before that occurs."

"Puter, is this signal always on?"

"Affirmative."

"Can you control the signal?"

"Affirmative."

"Can you shut it off?"

"Affirmative."

"Can I control it?"

"Remotely. By adjusting its intensity, you could shut it off."

"How come you've never shut it off?"

"You've never asked me to."

"Well, I'm asking you to shut it off now."

Whoop... de... do... Whoop... de... do... Whoop... de... do...

"Can you hold on a minute?"

"Incoming transmission from the desk of General George Keith, Martian Orbital Space Debris Recycling Service, Supply Clerk's Office, a.k.a M.O.R.A.S.S,..."

"Numan? That was really using your noodle. How did you figure all that out?"

"Figure out what? I was using my Random Thought implants."

"Incoming message. Downloading in three, two, one..."

"This is General George Keith calling from my desk, ah, in the future, and if I am talking to you two wisenheimers, Van and Numan, on Earth, that I sent out yesterday, aboard an orbiter, which I might add, you destroyed, and that you also destroyed a Chinese satellite, which had serious consequences in the future, when you left, in the past, I must be talking to you in the present, which is in the past. Is that right, Ship's Computer?"

"What? Affirmative. Even I'm in a time warp."

"Let's see, Van and Numan. Hmmm. You were supposed to report to me when you landed on Earth in the future, but that was in past. And I am here, now, on Mars, in the future, and you two whack-a-doos have been without an assignment – screwing around on Earth for weeks in the present. Right now, right?"

"We've been here right now for some time ago a while back then waiting a brief period in the present now for the moment, sir."

"Well, I am putting my foot down, right now. Your current reassignment orders will go on record tomorrow, which will be received yesterday, and go effect in two days. I am sending a transporter ship to collect you at future co-ordinances, set at RTS 3436, in the past, and you both better be on it today, or your ass is grass tomorrow. I've not forgotten it, but I must have said this before, since I say it now. This is General George Keith, signing out, officially last week, two days from now yesterday, good evening."

"Puter, any suggestions what we could do?"

"Since you've ordered me to shut off your Clone Domes, you could run amok, or work anonymously in a food related service industry in the past. Or you can get your ass back to Mars and get assigned to the barracks in the future, like the General said."

"What say you, Numan?"

"I say we split presently."

"Okay, Puter. Thumbs up, we stay."

"All this past present and future stuff has given me a tense headache. Let's book to the fish taco stand, and scarf down some righteous burritos and chips."

"Susan? Isn't Ramon's fish taco stand up the boardwalk?"

"Yeah, it's up a block or two. This might not be any of my business, but it sounds like you guys are in some heavy trouble. That General sounds confused and serious."

"Oh, he's always been an old hard on, but don't take him seriously. He's like a dad to us even though we never had one."

"Hey, let's look for seaweed on the way. I wanna make a hat."

"Yeah, I could use some new shoes. Bet I could make you a really cool dress, Susan. I can weave that stuff into anything rad."

"Look, a sand dollar – my lucky day. I'll buy lunch!"

"Puter? Turn up your gravity suspension mode, so you can keep up with us. Say, I was wondering? Could Typical Susan ever be transported into the future with us, like say to a C.L.O.D. orbiter or the tower apartments?"

"Negative. Typical Susan's presence in the future would cause a massive time-warp shift and shrink her to the size of a Milk Dud. Besides, the intense flash from the Transport would fry her like a bacon rind."

"But Puter, either way, we want to stay with Typical Susan. We could watch all our shows together, stay up late, and get up when we want to. Would it really disrupt the future even though we have nothing in common in the present?"

"It would surely suck for Susan to miss all of our future television shows. Wouldn't it, Susan?"

"I don't know. I guess it would be really cool missing all those re-runs. Plus, I would know what happens before anyone else. I could even bet on the lottery!"

"For sure, you know."

"Are you going to order for us, Numan?"

"Surely! Oh-la Taco Stand Man."

"Hey, dude. Don't I know you? What's going on? Can I righteously get you anything?"

"No problem. How about tres fish burritos, and tres Dos Equis, all around?"

"Ah, sorry for the hassle, dude, but I gotta see some I.D., for the brews? You understand, man? The Man watches anything Mexican."

"Surely, dude. We got Typical Susan. My crew and I just finished shredding some three foot swells north of the pier. Kinda glassy out there with clear walls and the break curls on the outside, towards the south end."

"Oh, really dude? Awesome! Is that where the break is today?"

"Yep, we were really stoked. We owned it."

"Righteous. I'm jetting up there when I clock off."

"Check it out! Cow-a-bun-GA."

"So, ah, let's see, where were we? Who is paying for this order, again?"

"Oh, Susan? Can you pay the brah? I only got a few shells and we are ever so short on cash-ola."

"Hey dude! Won't your little glass-head friend have a brew too?"

"Negative. I'll be flying with the fuel I flight."

"Alright then, Brah. Find a table and your order will be out, on-mo-mento pour favor."

"Grass-see-ass, Sen-yor dude, fish taco man."

"Van, maybe we could work here and eat all the fish tacos we can have?"

"Susan, thanks for paying. Can I give you a hug?"

"Sure! I'm down for that anytime."

"I'm not sure I am, but thanks again."

"Gee, I think I felt a little more than a hug there. I guess you're really happy I came."

"I guess I am happy you came too."

"*Holy shit, holy shit!!!* What was that?!!"

"What was...that siren blast?!"

"Van! Look over at the parking lot."

"Shit! Oh, no. It's a red transporter ship!"

"Oh cripe! My head is spinning! That blast, aaah, it goes again."

"Run, Susan!"

"Run, Van. Run, Puuuter!"

"Negative. My panels are frozen in green goo."

"Puter? Can you reboot?"

"Neegaatibbe."

"Thank heaven, Susan got away. I can't move my legs. Are you stuck to the ground? My arms are locked to my head!"

"I can't move anything either. My feet are boiling into the concrete."

"Why are we the only ones stuck here?"

"Stay where you are, Mister! Drop the brewski, and put your hands into your head."

"Ouchy!... Susan? Why are you back here in that totally rad and revealing paper uniform?

"What are you slime molds talking about? I'm Clone Officer, Susan. I was sent by General George Keith, from the clone sample patch 845.21, to transport you cretins back to Mars."

"We can't, we're frozen."

"Tractor beam off. Now drop and give me twenty. What's that on your chin, soldier?"

"Guacamole, Sir, I mean, Madam. I mean Officer Clone Susan, title 845.21"

"What kind of clone soldier has guacamole on his chin? Ah-ten-hut! Eyes front! Now, why do you, two Earth worms, have your Clone Domes shut off? Answer me!"

"Well, Van had a headache, and we missed our show today, but we wanted to order some griddle pans, or maybe some chef's knives, would have been nice. We went to the tide pool to see something weird stuck there. We want the other Susan back, but we were so hungry, and say? How did you find us?"

"The General set the transporter ship to these co-ordinances. Isn't this the parking lot at Ramon's Fish Taco Stand on south pacific beach? And hey, wait. You shall speak when ordered to and only then."

"Pah-leese! Stop poking me, it hurts."

"You boys are gonna be in a world of hurt, but just you wait until you get back to Mars. The hurt will change to pain. Real Martian pain. Is this a sorry-ass excuse for a C.L.O.D. computer? With burns and seaweed stains on its panels? Computer: Stand fast!"

"Affirmative. Oh, I'm fastly standing."

"Re-intensify and activate their Clone Domes, now!"

"Negative. I've had enough of you First Generation types, ordering me around. You must put in an order form first – FX .0024-H, which will over-ride the directive in Clone employee assignment Manual code 0056, page 5, part 3, which was submitted by clone employees, hither known as Van and Numan, in my presence, on the solar day of TH.,187. To null and void the previous submission-"

"Cut the crap, clod computer. Clone Officer Manual directive 1136, code 46, page 95, parts 4 through 7, clearly state the exceptions of Earth parking lots, and/or drive ways, and/or drive-ins, and/or motels, malls, in regards to Clone Dome re-activations."

"Sorry Van, Sorry Numan. Clone Officer Susan has a point there."

"What you spineless clones need is some discipline - my top-secret, private, tool calendar, discipline!"

"Ah! For two cents, I'd drop you like a bad habit."

"Now that's the kind of soldier we don't need in this man's...ah, clone's army."

"I know you are, but what am I?"

"Get on the ship! Or do I have to carry you on?"

"Go ahead. Try it. You might like it."

"I can lift you scum bags off like the garbage you are. Now close the door."

"Wow-we, Van, saaay, I really like these new velvet seats, and the blue wall paper pattern is really quite chic. It all nicely contrasts with the teal sheets and pillows in the sleeping module!"

"For sure! I like how they furnished the place with all my favorite shampoos, lotions, and essential body oils."

"Gosh, I feel so relaxed now that I can crawl into my beddy-by."

"Clod-ball computer? Wipe off the seaweed and get your butt connected to the inter-space drive panel. Download co-ordinances .0072 to the signal towers. Van, Numan,? Get out of your grubby clothes and into your paper transport uniform jammies, pronto."

"But you'll see our naked buff buns!"

"Even though, I'm a First Generation Pleasure Colony clone, I have zero interest in seeing your marshmallows. Now get going. I'll drive! Oh, by the way? Try not to ralph up your lunch when we get zipped through. The cleaning service clones really gag when they smell chunks. Also, there will be a high-ranking officer, directing you to your new living quarters, when we arrive. I don't know who, but General Keith is on vacation at the moment. Transporter ship: transporting in Three... Two... One..."

Flash!

Chapter 5

Earth

Past

"Van and Numan? The last time I saw them was a couple of weeks ago. It was a beautiful autumn night, with the Santa Anna winds blowing from the desert. I really felt good because my doctorate thesis on the economics of recycling orbital space debris was completed after months of hard research. After I submitted the thesis to the department chairman, a few colleagues and I, went out to celebrate at Don Ramon's, the local Mexican restaurant. While we were waiting for a table, I noticed a familiar face behind the bar, but I wasn't quite sure. After all these years, he hadn't changed a bit, except that his blonde hair was short and spiky. I had to make sure I wasn't seeing things, so I went up and ordered a drink...

"And what would you like, Madam?"

"A Bloody Mary, please. I am celebrating tonight."

"Puter? Mix one Bloody Mary for the lady."

"Affirmative. Do you want a celery stalk?"

"Yes, that would be nice."

"Would you like an olive with that?"

"No, that's okay."

"How 'bout a cocktail onion?"

"No, I don't want salsa here!"

"Do you want a hazelnut?"

"No, just a straight up, plain, Bloody Mary, please."

"Affirmative."

"That's quite a fancy cocktail mixer you've got there. Does it make all the drinks for you?"

"Puter? Yeah, he's done other things, but I re-programmed him to be my mixer now. We don't usually talk to patrons, but what are you celebrating?"

"My doctorate paper on the economics of recycling orbital space debris. It's finished, and I submitted it to the department today. I'm with some friends over at that table."

"In that case, Puter? Mix a couple of rounds for the lady's friends."

"Affirmative."

"Lady? I think I know a little bit about recycling space debris. I was once involved with a project..."

"How could you? This is a new science, that is just emerging. You would have to be either from the future, or part of the Chinese research team, to know what's being planned for missions to retrieve satellite material. Unless, well, maybe you are? You look very familiar, but I didn't know whether..."

"Typical Susan?"

"Numan?"

"You were the only Earth woman who could tell us apart."

"Wow. After all these years, you haven't aged a bit, even the little scar on your ear still looks fresh."

"I sorta remember when that happened, do you?"

"Of course! It was one of the most outrageous parties we went to. There was a local band, everyone was skinny dipping, it was a huge kegger. You were the life of the party until you saw the needle and passed out."

"I'll never let him try to pierce my ear again, ever!"

"So then, this must be Puter!"

"Affirmative. I was just trying to do my job with what I had."

"Where is Van?"

"He has a hard time talking to Earth people. They put him in the back, washing dishes."

"You'll have to tell him I'm here. I'll always remember the day at the taco stand, when the ship landed, but my memory of it is vague."

"Hey, keep it down, okay. There's Earth people around."

"What happened?"

"Clone Officer Susan, blasted you with a memory spray, just as you ran. That's why you can't remember it very well. And because the ship made such weird scorch marks, she also blasted the owners into thinking they should rebuild. This used to be the fish taco stand and now it's Ramon's Mexican restaurant. Clone Officer Susan was sent to take us back to Mars."

"How long were you gone?"

"I don't really know? It could have been years. With time warp travel these days? You can't tell where you are from a hole in the ground – all the transport time lag."

"What happened when you went back to Mars?"

"They awarded us with some medals, and I got a headache. We were put in some kind of a sleep lab, I think. Then they sent us back to

Earth without our Clone Domes 'cause they think we set off a missile, but we were only doing our jobs. We've been stranded ever since. Nobody knows we're here and nobody really cares. It's a real drag to be marooned."

"Is that what happened?"

"Well, they had an award ceremony for us..."

"Good evening ladies and gentlemen, distinguished representatives of the Martian Districts. Welcome to the Edgar Cayce Institute of Research and Development of Clone Esoteric Studies and Dream Manipulation. My name is Chairman Le Jour. Tonight, we wrap up this informative series of seminars on the general topic of how chance, randomness, and chaos, enriches and plays, such an important role in our lives. Last night, we were astonished when my colleague, Chairman Das Nacht, conjured up the spirit of John Cage. John looked good and was feeling his old self again. He was generous to speak to us about his process of using I Ching coins and chance operations within his music compositions. Tonight, Chairman Das Nacht concludes his insightful analysis on Franz Bardon's work, focusing primarily on Bardon's visions of the astral plane. Chairman Das Nacht will conduct his entire lecture while under a self-induced trance. He has, therefore, requested that all communication devices be shut off. Only he, will communicate, during this time. But foremost tonight, we are honoring Van and Numan with an award ceremony, presenting them with the Crimson Star of Bravery, our highest Clone Award given on Mars. Van and Numan are Seventh Generation clones, and I am honored to give you some context for their extraordinary achievement of chaos. As you well know, Seventh Generation clones were first bred as sexual servants, but their passiveness made sex with them as exciting as making love to a wet paper bag. Studies showed that clone women would twitch around distractedly, and clone men would lay passively uninterested. An eighteen year old clone had the sex drive and libido of a seventy year old earthling. We have found that the reproduction of clone DNA is analogous to a photograph being reproduced, over and over again, on a xerox machine. Physical details fade into a simple mass of contrast, and this is why their skin is as clear as a newborn baby. Because of this degeneration from gene reproduction, clones also possess a retro-grade purity. That is to say, with each generation, a purer form of a reversed physical modality would emerge, which had unusual physical side effects. For example, on one hand, their muscle mass and hair, grow thicker and more quickly, yet, they possess small genitalia. This was problematic for both genders: for clone women giving a more difficult birth, which we never really advised, and for clone men, the minor inconvenience of having to sit using the bathroom. Yet, for us real people, this physical alteration became an asset during sexual relations with them. Also, Seventh Generation clones rarely get colds and the flu, yet they are constantly irritated by minor conditions of ingrown nails, ingrown nose and ear hair, cold sores and paper cuts. Recently, we have witnessed many cases of gender alteration and re-alteration. The notion that clones could change gender spontaneously, and then change back again, was astonishing to us. However, we discovered many of these clones became too exasperated with their domestic decisions of who would wash the dishes, or what kinds of clothes to wear on a daily basis. Having said that, we then started shifting our clone intentionality from the sex trade to manual labor. With much more success than before, Seventh Generation clones were trained in a variety of occupations that suited our economy. Besides being self-delusional, easily confused, and emotionally stunted, these prissy clones developed into a formidable and sometimes competent class of volleyball players, waiters, surfers, and models. We, at the Edgar Cayce Institute, have found in our research experiments, that these clones are master dreamers, capable of extraordinary feats of clairvoyance, remote viewing, and lucid dreaming. We are currently *using* clones, I mean, *studying* how clones manipulate the dream space, in covert warfare operations. Van and Numan, served aboard a C.L.O.D. Space Debris Recycling orbiter, and are now in the service of covert dream studies, here at the Institute. We award them tonight for their bravery with the Crimson Star. This medal is awarded for their conduct in the face of great danger. They put aside their personal safety, by sacrificing their regenerated ship, in order to destroy a pesky Chinese satellite. This selfless act of bravery, not only advanced our ongoing effort to annoy the Chinese, but also destroyed the instrument that interfered with the transmission of our television shows. It simply got in the way, and caused too much white noise, static, and just plain lousy reception. Their orbiter, upon its reentry to the surface of Mars, also crashed landed on a fleet of Chinese all-terrain rovers, which were being used to run illegal supplies of exotic lotions and essential oils to the Pleasure Colonies. In conclusion, Van and Numan made the conquest of Mars less of a hassle, created chaos for the Chinese, and advanced our housing settlement effort by enabling clearer television reception. Also, I am proud to announce that Clone Dome reception is up twenty per-cent due to their actions. It's my pleasure and privilege to present the Crimson Star of Bravery to Van and Numan. Van? Numan?... Oh, Van and Numan? Clone Officer Susan? Where in the H E double hockey sticks are Van and Numan?"

"They are asleep, Chairman, sir."

"Well, this put a wrench into the works. I suggest you find them, and wake them up, so that we can get on with the ceremony, and pronto."

"May I remind the Chairman that Seventh Generation clones suffer from dream concussions if they're awaken from their slumber. Official dream army regulations from the covert Dream Code manual, state that stirring clones from their sleepy slumber, jars the dream eye to close prematurely, resulting in glitches in psychological dream alterations and damage to the..."

"Alright. *Okay!* Ladies and gentlemen? I apologize for the slip-up that Clone Officer Susan caused. She's a First Generation Pleasure clone, and the girl has got a lot to learn about order and chance. We will now, reluctantly, throw out the really neat award ceremony and continue with our dogmatic lectures. Put away your communications devices, and give a good round of applause, for my colleague, Chairman Das Nacht."

"Good evening, ladies and gentlemen. Most of you are familiar with my abilities and published research papers. I would like to begin my lecture tonight, by requesting that you all remain quiet, so that I can concentrate on falling into a deep hypnotic trance, in which I'll summon..."

The dream eye was already opened, when the sky was filled with a thousand constellations. Below, he saw Typical Susan, on Carson – the Tonight show, all wrapped up in ribbons – a "let me call you sweetheart," daguerreotype: "I have noodles for contact lenses," she sang out, "bet you can't conjugate that?" Carson and the audience howled! Susan continued, and they couldn't stop her. "Noodles, nudeless, nude-alls, that's using your noodle!" and she emerged as a Star in the watercolor sky – a cult favorite. Van, incongruously, walked out on stage, which was now raining silver confetti. Carson looked over with an expression of shock and irritation that someone would interrupt his show like this, and lit a cigarette."

"Van? Get your ass out of my dream!"

"But Numan, we always dream together and this fun!"

"This is my dream window and I haven't fully entered it. Now, get out, dude!"

"But Susan is here and we're on television."

The dream eye was closing, yet continuing... "Long ago, and oh so far away, I fell in love with you, before the second show. Your guitar, it sounds so sweet and clear..." He was now staring at a solar disk – a warm orb of starlight, diamond, within it's luminosity. "There is a light that never goes out." Drifting bodies across spiral galaxies away. Now, it seemed as though he saw her in a past dream, a dream within a dream, a shuffled-out playing card, a blonde angel grasping his hand, leading him away from something about something. Numan strained hard to remember her face, but it turned into a frail memory – a winter flower shivering under the snow. He was consoled by a feeling, looking at a row of street lights in central park, that a promise was made. "Maybe Typical Susan will call from the Tonight Show's green room..."

Whoop... de... derp... Whoop... de... derp... Whoop... de... derp... "Incoming emergency transmission from General George Keith to anyone, anyone?"

"Incoming emergency transmission from General George Keith to anyone, anyone?"

"Okay, okay! We're awake! And now, I've got a spinning headache. Why did you wake us up, General?"

"Hey you guys. This is important!"

"What do you want?"

"Van, Numan, help me. You must help me! No one answers me."

"Why is that, sir pickle face?"

"I am marooned on Titan – the moon of Saturn, and it's all your fault."

"What did we do now?"

"I was going to the Pleasure Colony on Phobos, when my ship's wing hit the edge of your damaged Collector Dish's Entry Armature Railing, or the tip of S.P.O.C.'s E.A.R., and sent it off course to Titan. I am stranded here. Fortunately, I met up with these two other characters, Unk and Boaz. They're good soldiers, with mechanical skills, but their antennas are driving me nuts! I command you to get me out of here, or at least, tell somebody I'm here."

"You can't command us any more, not after we got our neat Crimson Star for all our important and buff acts of bravery."

"What acts of bravery did you two morons ever do?"

"We bravely destroyed our ship, which bravely destroyed a bad-ass Chinese satellite and rovers, and bravely got sent back to Earth, then bravely back to Mars again, where we don't know who we are. Wasn't that brave?"

"Are you kidding? Why, in the *Sam-hill*, did they give *you* a medal? I've done many acts of bravery and they haven't given *me* any medals. In fact, even though my rank is a title, I only got one trophy – for the re-enactment of Spud-Nick."

"I guess it wasn't big enough, General."

"You two Clod-Hoppers don't deserve diddly-squat. You simply destroyed a valuable hardware ship, which accidentally destroyed a Chinese satellite and a few army robot rovers. And now, through your neglect of not completely destroying S.P.O.C.'s E.A.R., you've left a dangerous obstacle in our orbit, which changed the trajectory of my ship!"

"Well, wasn't that a brave thing to do? Chairman Le Jour says so."

"Listen up and listen good: Clone Manual Code Orders state that you must follow my orders, regardless of safety to yourselves and others. You must be nice to me when I'm hurt or in danger, and you must listen to me, and do as I say, so that the good of the people comes first in all cases, which the army so proudly serves. And when I get back to Mars, you're gonna be digging ditches and painting lawn rocks for the rest of your..."

"Can you wait on that, General? Chairman Le Jour and Clone Officer Susan just got here. Talk to them."

"Oh, how ya doing, Roi, er, Chairman Le Jour? Did you get my latest progress report?"

"Who is this?"

"It's me, George!"

"George, who?"

"General George Keith. I've been calling you and calling you. I've left urgent messages as to the status of my emergency. I am marooned here, and I outrank you. I command you to do something about this."

"Ah, yes, General George Keith. I've been waiting to talk to you. You managed to change the entire intention of my project, didn't you?"

"The Valhalla Project, sir? No, I kept it on track."

"I was expecting this from you. So, I'll be specific. You agreed, that this was to be an unmanned mission, didn't you?"

"Well, you never mentioned it would be a clone mission."

"Did you send Van and Numan up there?"

"They were supposed to be there for a couple of days, you know, routine maintenance duties."

"Yet, in addition to that, you sent up a Fifth Generation clone, who managed to disengage the Collector Dish, which wasted a lot of the ship's regeneration energy, and became the impediment that sent you off to Titan. Was that maintenance as well?"

"Rico was sent to speed things up. Yes."

"And none of the material collected was ever sent to the Institute?"

"I guess you got me there. But listen, Roi, part of it went into parts for building C Class rovers. It was a military contract, for heavens sake. Everyone got a piece of the action. Didn't you get one? We sent over a custom rover just for you. I've put my life on the line for this clone's army, and all I have to show for it, is a title, a few benefits, a lot of hash marks, and one lousy trophy. Don't I deserve a golden parachute and a few health benefits for my years of socialist service."

"Can't trust you, George. This project was for the good of Mars, with valuable minerals to be donated for long term generous grants and supplies, for students. I'm going to let the army deal with the rest of your business."

"So, you were gonna use everything for *your* Institute and *your* students?"

"I was the one who thought it up, and funded the damned thing."

"And all because the debris made us look like Saturn?"

"Spoiled my view of the Milky way, couldn't have that aura."

"And because of that, my ship hit an obstacle, which you designed?"

"Random things happen in space, all the time."

"It ruined my vacation. I am stranded here with other characters from other stories."

"Consider it a permanent vacation, George. I am turning off your transmission. Nobody will answer you. You're on your own with Unk and Boaz. We've got much more important and pressing business here with Van and Numan."

"My permanent Vaa-caa-tion!..."

- Click -

"Alright then, you good for nothing birds, stand in. Chairman Le Jour has a few words regarding your remote viewing progress and your next dreaming assignment."

"Thank you, Clone Officer Susan. Would you mind standing over there? Your skimpy paper uniform is a distraction right now, but we'll make adjustments for that later, in my office."

"Chairman Le Jour?"

"Yes, Van?"

"Numan and I are hungry. Numan has a headache and he doesn't look too good."

"Get a grip on it, Numan. Why do you have a headache?"

"I'm always hungry and talking to that General Mofo gives me a headache."

"Alright. Here's a chocolate chocolate peanut butter energy bar for you, and a toasted coconut vanilla strawberry-mint bar for Van."

"Could you change mine to chocolate chocolate peanut butter, too?"

"Sorry, Van, but your monthly allowance of chocolate chocolate peanut butter has expired. If you eat anymore, your muscle mass will expand to an under-performance level. I will, however, increase your allowance for lemon oatmeal banana."

"But that's got uno chocolate in it."

"Sir, why can't Van have peanut butter banana chocolate oatmeal?"

"That's got chocolate chocolate in it."

"It hasn't got as much chocolate as peanut butter chocolate almond maple."

"Could I do the oatmeal banana lemon with strawberry-mint

chocolate, then? That doesn't have much chocolate chocolate in it."

"Peanut butter is off! Now, take this pill with your energy bars. It will extend your dream period, allowing you to move more freely, and it will help you easily change the dream space, as you remotely view the scene."

"I think my head coming around with this."

"Good. Listen, I'm very proud of the progress and scope of your dream level. You are finally prepared to take on a more advanced mission. It will involve remote viewing. We suspect the Chinese are building a carbon reactor for their rocket fuel. They can easily alter this fuel for an explosive device that, when detonated high in the atmosphere, would knock out all communications to Clone Domes. Your job will be to enter the dream space, continue to the inside of their defense complex, and remotely view their plans. Clone Officer Susan will advise you, and show you her schematics of the building. She will enter your dream space, and guide you to the office, where we suspect the plans are. You must accomplish this in a timely manner, her dream energy can only be sustained for a short while. Your assignment starts right now. I must get back to the main room of the Institute for a tea leaf reading, so I'll leave you with Clone Officer Susan."

"Thank you, Chairman Le Jour, now boys, behave yourselves. You heard what he said. Looks like we've got a nocturnal e-mission with the Chinese. It isn't gonna be easy. Take a good look at my schematics, here. This is where the target room is. After we drink our sedation mixture, and fall into a stable altered dream consciousness, we will meet at the usual dream home meeting space. From there, we'll move to the target room and remotely view their fuel plans. Any questions? Yes, Numan?"

"Could you bend over more? I can't see all of the schematics."

"Sure. How's this?"

"A little bit more...nah...yeah, that's better. Yeah!"

"Numan? You have another question?"

"Yep. Will you sleep next to me and sing to me this time?"

"I suppose, if it will help you get off to dream consciousness faster."

"Oh, it will get me off alright."

"Clone Officer Susan?"

"Yes, Van?"

"Could you mark a line to the target room? 'Member how Puter marked a line to the escape pods so we could find out what we needed to do. It really would help us out."

"I can't do that in dream space. You'll have to follow me there."

"Clone Officer Susan? Why are you so much nicer when we go on assignments together?"

"I don't know. I guess it brings out my pliant side when the Chairman orders me around. Alright then, let's drink up, boys, and get to dream consciousness. We'll meet at the usual dream home. Good night, gentlemen."

"Susan? I like the way your buff body feels under your paper uniform, next to me."

"Somehow, I knew you were gonna say that, so keep your hard-on to your self, and turn over and get to sleep..."

The dream eye opened into another light for all of them. Van arrived at the dream home meeting space first.

"Geee, I love this old cabin in the woods every time I get here. The snow is so pretty falling up, with the starfish and little elephants playing in the transparent trees. It reminds me of those cute paintings I'd see in those *art gallery stores on Earth. I always wanted to buy one and hang it in the apartment. It would have brighten up the place. I really like the rustic furniture and all the rocks too.*

"Numan? Are you here yet?"

"Yeah. Turn you around. I'm over at the fireplace. I can view Clone Officer Susan in the cozy den, waiting for us."

"Hello, boys."

"Wow, Susan. Why are you wearing that little thong bikini, when you usually wear the cheerleader's outfit?"

"Do you like it? Thought I'd show you I don't always have to act lady-like. Besides, it will make it easier for you to follow me."

"What do you want to do with us, now that we're all here?"

"We'll move through the window and you'll see the red sands of Mars."

"We have to cross that? No wonder you wore that bathing suit. It's hot!"

"Too bad we didn't bring our long boards, we could have royally shredded some sand tubes."

"Okay boys, there's the Chinese defense complex. Move across the sands. If you see any Chinese dreamers out there, be careful and don't talk to them. They're bored and always love to chat. They'll get you caught up with some trivial nonsense and delay us, when we've got a mission to do. We need to go through the gates, through the red door on the right. See it?"

"Hey, Van? Try to keep up with Susan and I. And quit staring at her ass!"

"I can't help it, she's got such a royally stacked bod."

"Well, we managed to get by the dream guards – that was easy, they're always asleep in their dreams, anyway. Now, go down this hall, take a quick left, past the service desk, past the vending machines, make a right at the second hall, ignore the cute girl at the water fountain, enter the door on the left, through the curtains, and move to the left of the computer banks. You will then see two hallways. Go to the right, past the second desk, and you'll see the target room. Look at the documents in the fourth drawer."

"Gosh darn, Officer Susan, this place looked so much easier on your schematics."

"Why is this defense complex so dang big?!"

"Look, you guys, we're half way through this mission. I am running out of dream energy, and you have to remember."

"Susan? I think I am waking up. My real body has to go to the bathroom, and bad."

"Can't you hold it?"

"No, I'm really under pressure. Why did I drink *all* of that sedation mixture. I gotta go!"

"Alright then, Numan and I will finish the assignment."

"Tough luck, Van. Sorry you won't be a hero like me and Susan. See ya on the other side, dude."

"Van. Peeing out. *Later.*"

"Look, Numan, there are the curtains. Now, move to the left of the computer banks."

"Why is it snowing in here? My surfboard is knocking over the fire place and my transparent trees? Are getting heavy. I can't look sideways."

"Numan, can you look up and pull the edge of the dream scene with your hands?"

"I'll try, but the curtains are spinning, and I don't remember this pink starfish here."

"When was the last time you had a headache?"

"Let see? Oh, yeah, it was right when I was talking to General mofo."

"Was that right before Chairman Le Jour and I, came to your apartment?"

"Yes, I think so."

"Did his call wake you up from a dream?"

"I think so. I was looking at Van, and I thought he was waking me up, but my dream eye continued back to the scene I was having. Then, I heard a loud beeping sound and..."

"Shit! You're having a dream concussion. That explains the glitches in your remote viewing. Why didn't you tell us you had a headache?"

"I did."

"But you said it was from hunger – not from being disturbed by the General."

"I am hungry all the time, I can't tell the difference."

"We've got to get you out of here or we'll be trapped in this complex. If we get stuck here, it might take the rest of our lives, trying to remember who we are, and why we're here after we wake up. Use your sense of flying, so we can get back to the safety of the dream home quicker."

"How do I fly, again?"

"Use your will to feel sexual and then let go. I am losing dream energy, so I must hold on to you."

"Well that makes it easier, Susan. Look down, you can see the top of the defense complex. We're flying!"

"Fly across the red sands, and through the window, remember?"

"Say? Before we become lucid again, can I look at your thong bikini in front of the fireplace, and give you a hug? It would make my night e-mission."

"Sure, why not, I am up for that. I won't stop you."

"The firelight looks good around you, but my dream body is cramping up and losing energy."

"I can hold on to you, but I'm collapsing under this terrible weight."

"See you on the other side..."

He saw the brilliant white light flash, reddish, from under his eye lids. Then, a thousand stars, exploding into their ends

.

"Numan, wake up."

"Ouchy, my head hurts. Van, you know better than that. What a dream mission. What is it now?"

"Chairman Le Jour wants to see us. I think he's mad. I heard he already assigned Clone Officer Susan to the Out-land Pleasure Colony. Who knows what he wants to do with us?"

"Van, Numan, please report to my office immediately – through the side door, please."

"Aaah, come in, boys."

"Hi Chairman Le Jour. Say, heard any good jokes lately?"

"Are you boys alright? I mean, have you recovered from your dream mission?"

"Numan keeps seeing double vision flashes under his eyelids, and I can't tell what's real and what's not, most of the time."

"Well, that's normal. Do you feel different in any other way?"

"I've had a bad cold sore, but no, not really."

"Have you noticed that your Clone Domes are inactivated?"

"No. I haven't had a good high in ages, but you're the ones who'd know."

"Alright then, let's see. The both of you've been out of it for days, from the rigor of your mission."

"We're so sorry about that. We couldn't help looking at her stacked suit."

"Listen, it's alright."

"Are you mad?"

"Of course, not. Dreams are tricky situations. Things happen beyond our control. Despite our careful preparations, details get over looked, and things go wrong – the ghost in the machine, as it were. But are you aware of what happened while you were away?"

"No, not really, but we heard you sent Clone Officer Susan to the Pleasure Colony."

"Clone Officer Susan compromised her rank and position. Without a Clone Dome, she became sexually aware – that girl wants to do it with *everybody*!"

"Wow, I miss her already."

"Boys? Do you know what happen on your mission and why it was a failure?"

"Well, Van had to take a leak, the curtains were spinning, and the Chinese defense building was real big and confusing with different surfboards in the way, but the cabin was nice and the snow was pretty..."

"No. Not quite, son. Our fears of a Chinese bomb was confirmed. Hours after you left, the Chinese detonated a dirty carbon bomb in the atmosphere. The debris damaged the tower antenna, which disrupted communications to the Clone Domes of our worker clones. I'm now the supervisor of thousands of clones running amok. They think you caused this and see you as heroes for setting them free. But they're just as confused as you are. It's been a non-stop party for them ever since. It will take us years to get them under control, much less, put out the fires and clean the toilets."

"Whoa, our neat Crimson Star medals are nothing compared to this. Van, how's it going, hero dude?"

"I am sorry, guys, but we just can't have you around any more. It won't work out. You see, heroes and rock stars are a thing of the past. They controlled too many minds. It's just too dangerous these days to have someone around who's not what they say they are. It creates confusion for everyone, and gets in the way of randomness. You must undergo memory reorientation and be sent to Earth in the past – around the time and space that the General sent you. This way, nobody on Mars will know what you did or where you are. I am sending your assigned computer on the ship with you, but I'll have to clean its mother board, for safety sake. We can't let any future technology out of the bag. It'll be a little more capable than the Earth's robots at that time. You'll be able to program the computer for anything, however, I suggest you use him as a helper. You're gonna need it. Also, without an activated Clone Dome, nobody will track you. You'll be free to live out normal Earth lives. But in case you manage to really muck things up, I will install a emergency communications device in your Random Thought implants. Your ship awaits you at the usual launching area. Oh, and don't try any funny business. This ship is designed to dissolve minutes after you arrive. Good luck, gentlemen. I have nothing further to say..."

...Flash

"That's pretty much it in a nut shell, Susan. They've even erased part of our Social Memory implants, so it's really hard to talk or like anyone. I'm lonely here. Even Van doesn't want to work anymore. He's becoming more Earthly every day."

"Yes, but I listened. You can still talk to me."

"No. You can listen to me ramble on. I can talk at you, but not with you. I'm like an Earthling now, I am not interested in anybody."

"Well, that's very sad."

"Just think how we feel. We were like rock stars on Mars, and now we're just restaurant workers. Even Puter doesn't give us any respect. He's only interested in gaming. We're nothing here."

"But you still have your lives. You're young and haven't changed a bit."

"We both know that will change. Our bodies are changing already. We can't be reconciled."

"Even though I am middle-aged, I feel good about myself. There are so many things we could do."

"With what I get paid? You're set-up with a career. You'll want everything, all the time. All the time."

"I could find you something – another position."

"Look, it's closing time. I've got to get Van home, or he'll miss his continuing TV story about some survivor girl buying shoes in New York."

"But I'm still celebrating my paper."

"Your friends have all left the joint."

"I'll catch up with them later. What happened to the General? I still want to say hi to Van."

"I really don't think so. He thinks you could never tell us apart. It's late. I have to wipe down the bar."

"Can we still be friends?"

"I don't think we have much in common."

"I guess we really don't."

"Good night, sweet Susan."

Chapter 6
Chairman Le Jour's Office
Future

"Edgar Cayce Institute, Chairman Le Jour's Office. Can I help you, gentlemen?"

"Yes. Okay. Ah, yes? Aah, hello, ah, Miss Dix? Is it Miss or Ms. Dix?"

"It's Miss Dix, for sure. Can I help you?"

"We're here to see Chairman Le Jour. My name is Van. I was washing dishes, working in a restaurant on Earth. We worked there for ten hours. It was hard work, sweating in the hot kitchen, stacking all the plates up. I hated doing the silverware and the water was gross. We got an urgent message from our Random Thought implants. We came all the way from Earth. We didn't think we could come back to Mars to..."

Ring...Ring...

"Hold on there one moment, sir. Edgar Cayce Institute, Chairman Le Jour's Office. Oh yes! Hi, how are you? He said *what*? Oh no, did he *really*? I know! What? No way. Yes. *Yes*. That was *so* funny. I know. I laughed so hard I peed my pants. *I am so sure.* No way, really? Oh, *stop it*. *Really?* Yes. No. Huh...hummm. Oh, *did he?* Well, I'd never do *that*, I just couldn't. I know! It would be *so* awkward. Yeah. Huh? Really? Yes, yes, no. Listen, call me tonight. Bye. Bye. Gotta go babe, O.K.? Bye-bye... Now, what were you saying, sir?"

"We're here to see Chairman Le Jour. The water was dirty from the silverware. All the plates were stacked up, and we didn't get paid much. We didn't have a car. He sent an urgent message, I think? We didn't think it was him 'cause we couldn't come back to Mars but we did. We came all the way from Earth. We practically ran from Module 102 landing to make this appointment. We're not sure if we're supposed to be here on Mars, but the Chairman sent us a mess..."

Ring...Ring...

"One moment, 'K? Edgar Cayce Institute, Chairman Le Jour's Office. Ooh, hi, are you calling me back *again*? What? Yes. *Yes.* Oh, *stop* it. You know what I like. Of course, I *liked* it. I like everything you do. OK. Really? Oh, *shut* up! Yes. I know. Huh? No. OK. What? Yes. *I am so sure.* Yes, my panty hose? What? She was so dumb. Yeah. Why haven't you? Yes. No. *No. How gross!* I suppose I could later. I am so sure. She said what? *Really! I would*, maybe, if you'd. Huh? Alright, see you tonight. Bye. OK., I will. Bye. *Shut-up!* Yes. Yes. *Whatever.* Bye-bye. OK. **And you are?**"

"I am Numan and he's Van. We're here to see Chairman Le Jour."

"Do you have an appointment?"

"Yes, I think so. I don't know exactly. He sent us an urgent transmission. Could you please check?"

"Let me look that up, 'K? Oh god, let's see. Numan and Van... Oh, this dang old computer is running *so* slow today. Why is this dang old computer *so* slow?"

Ring...Ring...

"Good morning, Edgar Cayce Institute, Chairman Le Jour's Office. Can you please hold for one moment, sir? Okay, Mr Van and Mr Numan, Chairman Le Jour will see you shortly. Please have a seat."

"Is Chairman Le Jour in?"

"I really can't give out that information."

"Where is Chairman Le Jour?"

"He's over at the main room of the Institute. He's judging the finals of the Tarot Card Art competition, along with Chairman Das Nacht. Are you an artist?"

"No."

"Then take a seat. I have someone on the line, 'K. Chairman Le Jour's Office? Yes. Yes. I really can't give out that information. Are you part of the competition? Well, we had lots of entries. I don't know? The competition was really quite competitive this year. It was quite competitive, sir, really. Entries came in from all over the region. O.K.? *Really?* Would you like to come in and fill out an application? I really can't give out that information. He's over at the main room of the Institute, judging the finals with Chairman Das Nacht. Yes, you can call him over there. 'Bye."

"Say, Miss Dix? Are you a Seventh Generation clone?"

"Yes, I think so? Are you guys Seventh Generation clones too?"

"Yeah, how you can tell?"

"I could be your twin sister. You probably get that from every girl, huh?"

"Yes, but you're so pretty!"

"That's what Chairman, aah, never mind... I forgot. I really can't say."

"So, how fast are you?"

"What?"

"How fast can you type?"

"About 10 words per minute, if they're easy words. Last year, I came in second in the Miss Mars Receptionist Typing competition. See that ribbon over there? That's what I won. I am practicing real hard for this year's competition, but I won't make the same mistake I did last year."

"What was that?"

"Well, I was typing away, and I really got excited because I finished an hour before all the other girls. Then, after I downloaded my form, the judges said my fingers were on the wrong row. I was *so* embarrassed."

"Ouch, that must have really hurt."

"Yeah, the girl who won was from the ESP office. She thinks she doesn't have to do anything. She just sat there and filed her nails!"

"So, what are you gonna do?"

"Well, I've been working on my time. On a good day, when I have a 402 chocolate energy bar, I can almost do eleven words per minute. That's on a good day, with real easy words, like *at*. I don't know any other receptionist who can do five easy words per minute. Even the girl from the ESP office has trouble with *as*, *we*, and *did*. So, I'm quite confident I'll win this year, *if* I first look at my fingers."

"Wait a minute. How did you come in second? Wasn't your typing just a bunch of random letters?"

"I must have gotten a few words right."

"Say, is that a *virgin* oak desk?"

"Yep, pure wood. Chairman Le Jour bought it for me. He said his ESP said we needed a special surface for working on special projects. It's so smooth and glossy. You can slide right on it. I love the drawers. They're so roomy and smell so *good*! I can pack a lot of stuff in them. Wanna look in my drawers?"

"Ah, maybe later... Miss Dix? Have you ever had two at a time?"

"Excuse me?"

"Two calls at a time. What do you do when you have two calls at the same time?"

"Well, I can put both callers on the conference phone. If I can't do that, I'll hold one and please the other. Sometimes, I'm naughty, and push the wrong button to disconnect them. Sometimes, I'll just let them talk to each other, or pretend I can't understand them. It all depends."

"It all depends on what?"

"Whether I like them or not."

"Wow, I can see why the Chairman would hire you. I would hire you. You're hot!"

"Why, thank you. What is your name again?"

"Numan and that's Van."

"Well, thanks, Numan and Van. I forget clone names, but I'll try to remember yours."

"Is Miss Dix your *real* clone name?"

"No. Dix is short for Dixon."

"Is it easier to remember?"

"In some ways, yes."

"How were you able to change your real clone name? All the permission slips, and *everything?* Geez! You gotta be famous to do that."

"Well, I am. Dixon was my stage name. I changed it the moment I left Gusev. Whew, talk about a crater town! Way too dusty for me. After I worked there, I would never live in a mining town again. The Gusev crater is famous though, and I wanted to be famous. I think it was the landing site for the first NASA rover, back in... I don't know?"

"So, what did you do in Gusev?"

"I stripped for the miners, Silly. Talk about a bunch of chumps!"

"Oh yeah, there's a big Pleasure Colony in Gusev. Why did you leave that really cool job?"

"Well, one night, I was going for a big finish! A dusty old miner came up to the stage, looking in my costume, I grabbed the pole, swung around, and I kinda drop kicked him in the headlights. Knocked him out cold."

"Wow, you're a big girl. How high can you kick?"

"1.78 meters, but that's nothing. On a good night, I can reach 1.89 meters."

"That's totally awesome. It must have been a good night!"

"Yeah, I got fired the next day. I didn't mind – I just wanted to get out of there."

"Was that when Chairman Le Jour met you?"

"Noo! Chairman Le Jour is a gentleman. A real classy guy. He discovered me at the Diamond Dust club. He can read your mind, you know. I was drinking a Martian Sunrise at the bar when he read my thoughts that it was his favorite drink! He sensed using ESP that I was sad and needed deep therapy. He introduced me to meditation and staring exercises. Then he changed my Random Thought implants so I could chit-chat on the phone. Best of all, he switched my Clone Dome values, from a Pliant to a Promiscuous mode. Whatever that means. It's fun. It feels good! I can concentrate on myself now. I don't even twitch. That's a big problem for girls like me, in my Generation class, you know. It's so *good* now!

"Well, I'm glad you're enjoying yourself."

"So, aah, you look like nice boys. Maybe we could all go dancing? I *can* take two at a time, you know."

Blip. Blip. Blip.

"Miss Dix, are Van and Numan here yet?"

"I think so? They've been waiting for a while now."

"I've been here all morning with Farnsworth, waiting for them. Why haven't you sent them in?"

"Well, I've been taking phone messages. I put your pens in order. It's been so busy. I've told them about my ribbons, and cool dance moves. Weren't you judging the Tarot Card Art competition today? Are you mad at me?"

"Of course not, darling, I mean Miss Dix. The art competition was yesterday. Remember? Please send them in, honey."

"Wow, you guys must be important. Chairman Le Jour never gets mad at me like that. Please follow me, 'K?"

"I love the way you walk, Miss Dix! You move your hips so... Oh, Chairman Le Jour! Are we suppose to be here? We really didn't know what was going on."

"Come in boys! How ya doing? How many Martian years has it been – five, seven? Looks like you've been soaking up all those lovely Earth rays, huh?"

"Well, sorta. Earth was no picnic. It was hot and smelly. Taking the bus everywhere sucked. We ate in a damn taco restaurant every night. The towels and silverware were *so* gross. It's way too crowded on Earth. The wind is constantly blowing. Say, why didn't you answer our calls? We tried to..."

"Ah, give me a break, guys. Lots going on here. We've expanded our curriculum. Palm Reading enrollment is up 30 percent along with Tea Leaf Reading. There's Tarot Card Deck Rebuilding sessions, and Competitive I Ching Coin tossing. All that doesn't include Astrology reassignments or Intro to Dream Manipulation courses. Besides, you disconnected the emergency *emergency* communication drive in your computer when you reprogrammed it to mix drinks. Now, how could I've helped that?"

"Well, you could have helped us. We missed you. You could have sent Clone Officer Susan to keep us company and do our house work. The clothes dryer kept eating our socks at the laundromat. No Earth girls would *ever* do that. They want everything all the time. All the time. We couldn't make enough money for them to even *look* at us."

"Cool it, cool it. What if I were to say that things are gonna change? I mean, in a major way. Listen, are you guys hungry? Help yourselves to these sandwiches. They're leftovers from the Tarot Card Art competition. We got tuna fish, peanut butter, egg salad, and a lot of other goodies here. It's all real imitation Earth food, not just smuggled from the Pleasure Colony, either. You boys chow down, put your feet up, chill for a while."

"Thanks, Chairman Dude. You got some Shoe-She? I missed Japanese Wasabi already."

"Sure. There's lots more leftovers where that came from. So, guys, I suppose your Random Thought implants are going nuts, wondering why I called you back. First, I'll try to answer most of your questions. Then, this gentleman, here, Mr. Henry Farnsworth, will take over. Well, I'm really sorry we parted company the way we did. It was quite a rude send-off on my part. I'll be the first to apologize for that. But rules are rules. And without rules, there isn't any disorder. And without disorder, there isn't any chaos. And without chaos, hell, I'd be out of a job. Do you get what I am saying?"

"No, not really, but we get the chaos part."

"Let me put it another way. After you left, we had to wait three months for the booze and sex to run out on that little party you started. Everything had to settle into a stupor before we could issue new Clone Dome values. Even I got caught up in the madness, but that's beside the point. Looks like I made a serious error with you boys, sending you back to Earth. But, I have my Extra-Sensory perception, and I was only following it when I was forced to make a judgment call. So let bygones be bygones. Let me be the first to say... Welcome back to Mars, Gentlemen! And you are gentlemen. You've been awarded medals for your service aboard the C.L.O.D. orbiter. You both served well on your Remote Dream Viewing missions for the Institute. Our covert war with the Chinese wouldn't be going as random without your contributions. I am so proud of you. You should be proud of all your accomplishments. However, institutions can get arbitrary at times. Everyone is doing whom and nobody knows who's doing it. Somehow, in the rush to delete your files, we missed a few compensations that were due to you, at the time I, aah, *we* sent you back to Earth. It seems, a very important clause in the Clone Labor manual concerning your back wages, vacation time, and assets, was disregarded. We were under external pressure, guys. Things happen. Surely, you can understand that?"

"Chairman Le Jour? What does this all mean?"

"It means, in effect, that we owe you and Numan, a shitload of money. Consider yourselves loaded, boys! Now that I let the cat out of the bag, I am going to hand it over to Farnsworth, here. Mr. Farnsworth?"

"Thank you, Chairman Le Jour. Good afternoon, Van and Numan. My name is Farnsworth. Henry Farnsworth - the third, of the Los Angeles' Farnsworths. Gentlemen, I have here your portfolio containing all your assets and compensations. After careful analysis, I must say it's quite impressive, even by my standards. It's a handsome portfolio – a real high flyer. I assembled it personally, with all the ribbons and bows attached. Actually, I am the auditor who discovered the discrepancies in your accounts. Indeed, I've made it my job to follow your financial activity for some time now. I'm a S.C.A.M.R., or Special Clone Auditor Managing Representative from S.C.U.M., or Special Clone Union Management. I am here to advise you on your pending financial gain matters. So, think of me as your special and trusted friend. Now, do you have any questions?"

"Tell us more what Chairman Le Jour was talking about being loaded."

"Yeah, and how do *we* trust thinking of *you* as a special friend?"

"Oh! My goodness me. You boys are an anxious bunch. Now, now, wait, gentlemen. These financial benefits are available to you in time, but not all of your assets are liquid. You own mineral rights that extend over a large portion of the Olympus Mons. We also discovered that you, somehow, were awarded a copper mine in the Argo crater. These mineral rights were granted to you, based upon the location of your natural clone birth. Some of these assets are tied up in long term accounts. They were awarded after you completed your Remote Dream missions. Financial instruments, such as stocks and bonds, were invested on your behalf by S.C.U.M. These assets are just partial payment for your years of service aboard the C.L.O.D. orbiter. Some of your stocks were quite aggressive building capital. They matured exponentially, and awarded special dividends. The payouts were quite large. It so distressed me to find myself in the position of integrating the avalanche of cash flow on your behalf. I even resorted to the slimy venture of Chinese money laundering. Even so, you have many other assets that we're still in the process of evaluating, gentlemen. All this would be credited to you at the time they become exposed. However, on the other hand, let's just say you wanted to cash in your portfolio at this time. I would advise against this. The following actions would allow huge sums of property to exchange ownership. This would effectively crash the Martian economy. We wouldn't want that? Now, would we? We can, however, merely offer you anything you want as compensation, but you must really consider it. Think hard about what you want as an initial payment. Take a moment, if you could have anything, what would it be, Gentlemen?"

"A glazed doughnut!"

"Oh, I am touched by your sincerity and modesty. However, please consider a larger world view."

"How 'bout an Ion Blaster gun!"

"Hmmm...you've kept quiet up to now, Mr Numan. What would you like, sir?"

"I'm still thinking, but an Ion Blaster would be nice."

"Oh, very well! Let the record show, that the distribution of Ion Blaster guns, were implemented this day, under grave reluctance. The racket scares the hell out of everyone, but they're harmless to most people. Now, gentlemen, please consider more choices. All your assets await!"

"Look Van, we's packing!"

"I thought we only got one choice, you mean, we get another?"

"Why, yes, sirs. I must insist you think larger with your options this time. Certain percentages, must be made, to qualify certain conditions."

"Oh, god, let's see. How about Miss Dix?"

"Now you're using your noodle and thinking big! That's a tough one though. Unfortunately, she has too many personal issues. That girl is complicated."

"Dang it!"

"Gosh, I haven't thought this hard since we flushed our ship out to space like those mean aliens on Star Trek! Think Numan."

"I am. I am."

"I know! How about a silver plated deck of tarot cards?"

"Think larger, sirs. Perhaps, on a global scale?"

"Free psychic advice for a year?"

"Look, boys, I can see that Farnsworth, here, is running out of patience. I think I have something that will settle all of this, but you must trust me with your decision."

"Will it be better than a new, two-way, radio wrist watch?"

"Boys, I guarantee it. First, Farnsworth has some papers for you to sign."

"Thank you, Chairman Le Jour. Gentlemen, I have financial release contracts for your consideration."

"What do it say?"

"Oh, just petty details. They're just legal papers, turning over all your rights and assets to the Edgar Cayce Institute, in the event, anything would happen to you. Also, it will give my office full authorization and custody, to reinvest, dispense, or deny your assets, upon your demand."

"What do it mean?"

"Well, I could give you money, if you'd ask in a certain way. But that's always a risk, isn't it? Should you feel a discrepancy with this arrangement, you can always file a grievance law suit."

"Does that mean we'll have to get different clothes? Please translate, Farnsworth, pronto!"

"Well, you could sue the Institute and the Martian Federation for their shirts. But court costs, time, is spent better partying. Wouldn't you both agree? You have us by the balls as it were. So, let's be friends, and take the easy way out, *okay*?"

"Boys, *please*. Please listen to Farnsworth. He's trying real hard to get you through this. Forget about it and let's get this party started. I *do* have something special for you."

"I don't know? Getting a special suit from the Martian Federation doesn't seem like much. Can I just see what you've got behind Module door number three?"

"Yeah. What's with this special party shirt you've got going on?"

"Wonderful! I knew from the moment I met you, that you boys were sensible. We can all work this out together. Now, please sign this...and this...this one just initial...sign this, and this."

"Oww! This writing bugs my hand, totally!"

"Just a few more, gentlemen. Sign this...this...and this...initial one more here...and this...one last initial here..."

"Farnsworth? Can we wrap this up? I've got to throw a whole pile of I Ching coins to prepare my answers for a meeting tonight. And I know that you have to consult your astrological chart this afternoon, to determine what you'll have for breakfast tomorrow. So, can we get this ball rolling?"

"Yes, we're quite done here. Thank you, gentlemen, for your patience in these business matters. I'll proceed in processing these documents directly. It was interesting doing business with you. If you need me, you can contact my office through Chairman Le Jour, but please, only if you need me. I'd rather not converse, in any way, with you again. Good day, gentleman."

"I'm glad that's over with. All this legal crap gives me a royal hand ache. Chairman Le Jour? Can you show us what you've got now?"

"Yeah, what does it have?"

"Follow me, please. Try not to touch anything along the way. Just through this Module warehouse door, here."

"Oh, my god! Oh, my god!"

"It's all yours, boys. I hope you're pleased."

"That is awesome!"

"This is for us?"

"Yep, it's all yours. A brand new, Mercenary Bends, C Class Martian rover! Go ahead and check it out. It's fully loaded."

"It's everything we ever wanted and more!"

"I used my most advanced psychic ability to get it, even before you came back to Mars."

"Is that how you *knew* candy apple red was our favorite color?"

"Of course!"

"Are those real leather seats?"

"Yep, pure plastic."

"I really like how the tinted solar windows match the gnarly fat tires. It's totally pimped out."

"Extra cost. You boys are worth it."

"You're the best Chairman ever!"

"I've always extra-sensed that I was. Take it out for a spin. It's all ramped up and fast. It can top out at ten kilometers per hour. So take it easy on those craters, boys. Look, I even installed a new R computer. The codes are on the front dash. Have fun with your new toy, and I'll see you later."

"Alright! Slide aside Van, and let me drive."

"Oh, I guess so. It does look a little too mechanical. I'll watch you drive for a while, but you gotta let me drive around the crater."

"Sure, when we get there, you'll drive all you want to."

"Something tells me we should go to the Gusev Pleasure Colony."

"Sounds like a plan, man. R Puter, what do you think?"

"Affirmative. A Pleasure Colony is quite a wonderful vacation."

"Well then, program the Martian Global Tracking system to Gusev Pleasure Colony, and let's be off."

"Affirmative. Checking files. I think I'm showing the Gusev Pleasure Colony was recently located at 42.2 North by 89.7 West. You can never be sure with all the dust blowing."

"R Puter? Please start our new candy apple rover, like now."

"Negative. C Class rovers must be started manually."

"Geez, R Puter, what does that mean?"

"You must press down on the third shifter, while moving the second lever toward you, turn the far dial to the left while programing 1803, and step lightly on the fuel pedal."

"We did all that? Of course, it won't start."

"R Puter? What is the fuel level?"

"My sensors indicate solar fuel cells are fully charged."

"O.K. Let's get this puppy started!"

"R Puter? It won't start. Can't you over-ride manual ignition?"

"Negative. C Class rovers must be started manually."

"Why can't you start it manually?"

"Dang it, Numan, I am a R computer not a robot! Excuse my French. I'm just a second generation rover computer designed only to give instructions. You must press down on the third shifter, while moving the second lever toward you, turn the far dial..."

"Stop, stop, I've had enough of your weenie-whiny voice, with all your stupid directions today. You're out!"

"Well, if that's the way you treat all your R computers, I'd rather not interface with you either. I can find another, more nicer, operator than you, any day. R computer signing off."

"What are we gonna do now?"

"I think Farnsworth ripped us off."

"Maybe we should sell it?"

"Who would want this piece of junk?"

"Numan? Let's push some random buttons and see if it'll start. 'Member how we programed the television remote on Earth? We got that to start by waving it."

"Alright. Push some levers. I'll jiggle the steering wheel."

"Listen?... It almost started."

"Keep jiggling the steering wheel. I'll wave these levers."

Surr-rumm Surr Suurruum!

"Ha, we're in business!"

"How did we do that?"

"I guess we jiggled it off, but don't stop, we might not get it started again."

"Van? Get me on the loudspeaker: *Open Module 55 warehouse doors! Stand back. We's blasting off on vacation!*"

"Gee, that loud speaker on top is really loud!"

"Yeah, the Chairman didn't miss a thing. We can royally chat with other rovers now. This is totally styling. R Puter programed the co-ordinances already. It's up to the rover now. So let's sit back and chill."

"What do we got for tunes?"

"Looks like programed muzak from the C.L.O.D. orbiter."

"That will drown out the engine. Won't it? That's not good."

"Well, *duh!*"

"See if we can get in College Earth radio. They play all the latest tunes."

"Check it out! Our seats are moving with the bass."

"I wonder what the Pleasure Colony girls are like this year? Gee, I hope they're fast."

"If they're anything like Miss Dix, we're in for quite a night."

"What are we gonna to say to them? You know, it's hard to get them alone."

"I'd say I've got a neat C Class rover outside. Or. Would you like to see it?"

"I never thought of that. What if they want you to buy them a drink or a new dress?"

"No problemo. 'Member? We got cash. Look at this, Farnsworth gave me a big roll of tens. We can even go play gambling. Didn't he give you any money?"

"Sorta. Just his spare change - what he had in his pockets, and this paper that says IOU. Whatever that means."

"Well, you'll have to ask him when we get back. 'Sides, I can lend you what all you can have."

"Numan, can't we go any faster then 5 kilometers per hour?"

"Yeah, we could, but you would lose your teeth on this rocky road."

"I don't see any roads."

"Precisely. One boulder to our axle and we're in a world of shit. Let's just play it safe, and keep our safety belts on, just in case of turbulence."

"This strap totally cramps my style, dude. I can't groove to the tunes."

"Just let the seat do the moving and the straps do the grooving."

"You know, Van? I've been thinking..."

"What's that, my faithful Clone Bro?"

"I kinda miss green trees and lakes, like they have on Earth. I like the red rocks and gravel, but why so much of it? And why is there red dust everywhere – it's like it's on everything?"

"Yeah, I was thinking the same thing. Everything's so red here. But look on the bright side, bro., Earth doesn't have any craters like Mars. We own a whole mine here. I wouldn't want to go back to Earth and mix drinks after this."

"Speaking of craters, aren't we 'posed to go west at Williams Port crater? Why does that sign say Williams Berg crater?"

"R Puter? Shape up! You're back online. If you give me any more crap, I shall delete your sensory files, pronto. You won't know who you are from a hole in the ground. Now, why are we at Williams Berg crater and not at Williams Port crater?"

"Affirmative. Dang it! You interrupted my long interface with a really smart Martian phone app. I don't like being offline either. I need to know what's happening. Will you turn that music down? I can't hear my circuits think. Let's see, where were we? Oh yeah, can you give me a visual?"

"Open Visual Sensory panel. *Look*. See? We just passed a sign that said Williams Berg crater. Aren't we 'pose to be going west at Williams Port crater?"

"Are you facing the sun?"

"Yes."

"Well then, I think you're going west. Keep going, and eventually, you'll get there. Wherever you're going."

"You know where we're going - to the Gusev Pleasure Colony, 'member? You locked in the co-ordinances, didn't you? I think we're lost."

"How can we be lost when we haven't arrive yet?"

"We haven't. I commanded you to program the co-ordinances to Gusev, and you were 'posed to enter 14.7 South by 184.6 West."

"Checking command files... You just told me we're going west. Hold on one moment, please. Incoming urgent music download from the Martian Federation antenna. I gotta take this one, boys. Will be a while. It's a gigabyte from the seventies!"

"I should really crash that R Puter one of these days – useless piece of..."

"Look Numan, there's a little candy cane striped building in the distance. Maybe they can help us?"

"Yeah, I wonder if it's a sentry house. I can see someone's there."

"Pull up, dude."

"I say, my good man. Which way to the Gusev Pleasure Colony?"

"Greetings, Big Boy. You crossed the red line. You're in big trouble! We captured you."

"What? No way! We captured *you*."

"Nooo. We captured you."

"How can you capture us, when we're in our rover?"

"No. Now, wait a minute. You crossed the red line. See it here? We are the Chinese Sentry Guard. We guard Chinese Territory. How can you capture us, when we're on this side of the red line?"

"We didn't see any red line, so, we captured you, with our rover!"

"Yeah bro! Wouldn't you rather say, it's a faint, rust-colored line, on the burnt sand?"

"Yeah! How do you know it's even there? It could be some kind of gravel formation or even a mirage."

"Tough bounce on you! Look closer, Joe. The red line's here.

O.K.? It's always shifting, but it's here, somewhere. I know. We watch it every day. You're captured now. We got guns. It's okay. Okay? You come into our really neat guard house for a while and become chill Chinese. It's fun! Please park your Big Boss Rover. Come inside the guard house, now."

"Oh, and remove your shoes when you enter, rude American China-dude."

"Wow, Van, these guys have class; walking around in those glittery pointed slippers."

"I love the powder blue walls and the red tile floor."

"You guys get comfortable in guard house, see. Put on these silk robes over your grubby uniforms. The orange and green flowers show ancient Chinese respect in the temple."

"These costumes are rad! I feel all Sheik, royally."

"Look at these weird dragon pictures, the imported lotions, and expensive incense. I love jasmine incense! Can I have some?"

"Sure, boy. It will make your rover smell good. The girls will marry you."

"What are these dragons pictures for? Are there dragons on Mars? There must be, with all these pictures of them."

"Yes. We take many lucky pictures of mighty dragons. If you have a camera, it will bring you special luck."

"We'll need one for the Pleasure Colony, for sure."

"Yes, American Joe. Just look for the red light in the window and take a money shot."

"Say, why is this couch covered in plastic?"

"It's still comfy. Yes? Plastic keeps off the sand. Keeps it shiny new. It's a good thing."

"Then, it must be, a truly good thing."

"Gosh, Van, it's a good thing they know everything!"

"Oh, *no*, no. I've forgotten my Chinese manners that I'm most humble to learn. Please, share with me and my simple companion. My name is Vang and this is NuMing. What are your most honorable names?"

"I am Numan and this is Van. We are from the Cayce Institute. We worked aboard a C.L.O.D. orbiter for a while, then we got sent to Earth. We worked in a Mexican restaurant and had to take the bus everywhere, which was really boring, then we got sent back to Mars. We really don't know if we're 'posed to be here, but we own some kind of loaded mine, and we could have changed our suits, so we went on vacation and..."

"Okay, okay, cut the crap. We guard Chinese territory. We're bored too, but we'll make a party now. Okay?"

"Say, you guys speak really good English. What's with that?"

"Nooo, we are speaking Chinese. You are speaking Chinese too. What's with that?"

"No, we're speaking English. I am not speaking Chinese. You are speaking Chinese."

"No, I can understand you because you are speaking English."

"I thought you were speaking Chinese."

"I am, but I am translating it into English."

"If I am speaking Chinese, then you're translating it into English as you speak?"

"I am, but you just said you are speaking Chinese, and I can understand you. So, I really don't have to translate it into English. Oh, never mind, I like you guys. You look good in royal costumes. You look very familiar. I can see you now."

"You must be Seventh Generation clones with Clone Domes?"

"Yes, with ancient Chinese Domes."

"I thought so. Your Chinese blonde hair and pale blue eyes, give it all away."

"Yes, an old Chinese proverb on the wall says: We think you are cloned from us. You think we are cloned from you. Nobody knows who was cloned from whom."

"Was that an ancient Random Thought, Vang?"

"Yes, there is much wisdom in ancient Random Thoughts, so let's cut the crap, and make a pretty good party now, okay? Aren't you guys hungry? We have lots of good food. Lots of different kinds of tofu. Today is Tuesday, so, we just have strawberry coconut chocolate banana almond tofu. We love 'em, and of course, root beer."

"Root beers, all around!"

"What's in this root beer? I am getting a buzz on."

"There are roots, and very rare stems, brewed in our ancient root beer. It is most rare, but nothing you can't handle, American Chinese boy."

"I don't know why I was randomly thinking you'd have some rice, too?"

"NuMing, do we have any rice?"

"Nah, only for special occasion."

"No rice, just tofu today. Okay? It's good! This fun tofu is a rare specialty of the Cangwu Crater Province."

"Are we in the Cangwu crater now?"

"This is special tofu."

"I'll have to give our R Puter a good talking to."

"Hey Numan, this *strawberry* coconut chocolate banana almond tofu is really *fun*! It tastes like roasted garlic."

"Hoo-ray! Another American wins the special prize for guessing our secret ingredient!"

"Yes. Our secret ingredient is real imitation flavor. We can imitate anything. The Chinese love everything: Federal American Regional Territory."

Fah-foom!

"Oopies. Sorry about that."

"Ah Boy. You made a big hole with your Ion Blaster gun. That's not good. It needs to be higher for a window."

"Geez, I must have left the safety off."

"Well, the breeze feels nice on our feet, but it needs a good frame with curtain decoration."

"We gotta keep the new guard house window looking real buff, dude."

"Dude? How 'bout another round of root beer, dude?"

"Dude, is it me or is it you? Please stand up straight. Root beer makes you a very doofy Martian Chinese American. Very careless with your Ion Blaster gun. If you're ever gonna be a good Chinese..."

"What the hell is in this stuff?"

"Dude, so many wonderful swirling colors to drink, dude."

"Dude, we are having a very loud fun party with our happy drink, dude."

"Dude? Can we look at your Big Boss rover now?"

"I don't know, NuMing? It's a bit complicated."

"You think it's too complicated for a Chinese Territory Guard?"

"No, I didn't say that."

"Well then, your Martian rover looked real sharp, Joe. We just want to look at it for a while."

"You should see the Luxury Class rovers the Pleasure clones ride. This is nothing compared to those machines! They have all the extras. Say, we're going there. Do you want to come along?"

"No way, Brah. Our job is a real important big-time job. Besides, we are expecting the General soon. We gotta paint some rocks to fill in the red line. We'll be in major trouble if it's not filled in this time."

"Yeah. Was he mad when we tried to sweep it away when he wasn't looking."

"Look, forget about it. We gotta stay around, okay? Let's go check out your rover, dude."

"Okay, okay, no pushing. It's just parked over there."

"Check out this fine detailing, Vang."

"Very smooth, Joe."

"And these racing decals?"

"Sure, looks very sharp."

"These NASA retro-tread tires? It was real smart when they recycled space debris to make these Dubs."

"Yeah, Boy!"

"Can this Class C rover go over 2 kilometers per hour like Chinese rovers?"

"Yes, NuMing, and more! It was *real* smart of NASA to put in C45 twin hydro-cell batteries. This monster can top out at 10 kilometers per hour."

"It must really book!"

"Are these real leather seats?"

"Yep, pure imitation. They were *real* smart to use these fabrics on the interior panels."

"Very smooth looking!"

"And wasn't it *real* smart to put on a fresh coat of non-rusting, candy apple red, paint? This *smart* paint protects the rover from any bookoo dust storms; these *smart* solar windows have royal protection from the..."

"Okay, okay! You think you're *so* smart. You know everything. Which came first, the chicken or the egg? Answer the question, Joe!"

"What? I don't know... What?"

"The monkey. In the Chinese calendar. Okay? Answer the next question, smart boy! What does a man do standing up - a lady sitting down - and a dog do on three legs? Answer the question quickly, Joe."

"I don't know, shake hands?"

"Wrong. They're all talking on the phone! Now, who can kick higher, Vang or Van? Winner takes pink slip. I will measure, okay?... *Okay*. So, *big deal*. You both can kick at 1.75 meters."

"You forget we're all Seventh Generation clones with equal abilities."

"Dang it! Okay? It's fun!"

"The party's over, dude. Let us drive your Martian rover Class C."

"Well, I don't know. It's voice activated."

"I can imitate your American Chinese voice. We can copy anything, 'member?"

"We will drive your rover. Now!"

"Well, geez guys, I think we gotta get back to the red hills. It's getting kinda dark. We really liked the plastic on your furniture with all the free incense. I think the new hole, I mean, window, is a fine addition to your guard house. Van had a little too much root beer, and I'm really getting hammered. These costumes are neat, though."

"We want to!"

"I think you would really like the rovers at the Pleasure Colony better than this."

"No, we like *this* one."

"It's a bit technical to start once it's been sitting for a while. Are you sure?"

"Numan? I am beginning to think you don't want us to drive your new cherry Class C rover. Could I be wrong here?"

"Well, guys, I guess you see right through me. On any other day, I'd probably say..."

"Yes! Your eyes say no, but *our* guns say yes! Put your hands inside and under your head. I shall take over this candy-apple Bends C ride."

"We will enjoy driving away from you now."

"Hey Vang, look at all this fancy shit in here - lights, cameras, loudspeakers, even a robot arm!"

"Oh geez, Numan. I didn't know that's a robot arm? All along, I thought it was a hood ornament."

"They'll never get it started. 'Member, how we had a hell of a time jiggling it off. I still don't know how we got it started."

"Yeah, that's right. Ha-ha! They'll never figure out R Puter. They're in for it. We'll just sit back and watch them sweat."

Surr-rumm Surr Suurruum-rumm!

"Wait. How did you get it started?"

"I just pushed the red button, Joe."

"Hey, hey, don't gun the engine, you'll use up the transmission!"

"Sorry boys, but you never got this thing off. We're gonna find out what it's made of. Maybe we'll tell you – maybe not. See ya later, dudes."

"Can you at least? Aah, there they go. They probably won't call us on the loudspeaker."

"What are we gonna do now? These guys might think we're their replacements and not come back."

"Oh, they'll come back. 'Member how he said they couldn't come with us because they had an important job? We don't know how to paint rocks. They've got to come back."

"Look, they're doing wheelies up that crater!"

"Oh, no, they bounced off that boulder, big time."

"Look at them, flying over that sand dune."

"It's like a Chinese Fire Drill out there."

"NuMing better have his seat belt on, after he tore that door off."

"How are we going to pick up Pleasure girls with a wrecked piece of shit like this?"

"I don't know, but NuMing is out on the hood. It's like he's surfing up there."

"I thought he was driving?"

"He was. He's got the thing on automatic pilot now."

"Look, Vang is out there too. Ahhh, watch out for that rock formation!"

"That's gotta hurt!"

"They're gonna roll it if they take that weird boulder again."

"I am sure Chairman Le Jour installed a roll bar, he thought of everything and he made sure we'd..."

"Why are you two out of uniform? Drop and give me twenty! AH-ten-hut! Eyes front. Now, why aren't you two Martian Worms guarding your post? Is that tofu on your silk robe, mister? What kind of a soldier leaves the red line? I see that you've been doing a little house cleaning with that new hole decoration. There's root beer stains and tofu everywhere! Well, maggot, you're going to be doing a lot more cleaning in the Red Guard Barracks if you don't get back to your post. Now, what do you have to say for yourselves?"

"Excuse me. Sir? I think you're barking up the wrong tree."

"Well what tree am I barking up then, soldier?"

"First of all, after we take these robes off, you'll see that we're not soldiers. We're civilians. Who just got lost. We didn't mean to, but our R Puter somehow programed the wrong co-ordinances in our neat new C Class rover. We're from the tower region. We thought that the line was rust colored and we were 'posed to go to Williams Port on our way to the Pleasure Colony in Gesev. Then our R Puter said he wasn't a robot and couldn't manually start our rover. So please take it easy. Okay?"

"So, you're civilians, *aay*? Why didn't you say so? Geez, you let me go on like that? I could have busted my gut or something. Say, you boys speak good Chinese for being from the west. Are you hungry? I think there's rice in the guard house, and some tea too. Please, here, let me shake your hands. My name is General Tso's Keef. What are your good American names, if I may ask?"

"Sure, I am Van and this is Numan."

"It's a pleasure to meet you, Vang and NuMing. I got a couple of sentry guards around here named NuMing and Vang. I suppose your Seventh Generation clones like them. Look, I like talking to Chinese American Martians, we've got lots to talk about. Let's make a move to the guard house and sit for a while."

"Don't you want us to take our shoes off?"

"Nah, our pet robot maid sweeps up every hour. We like to keep the guard house in ship shape."

"Shouldn't we put these really cool robe costumes back on? As a sign of respect for the temple?"

"Nah, way too formal. Your official uniforms give you lots of respect. Too bad you don't have American cowboy boots."

"I once had on big American cowboy boots, when I played loud, in a rock band."

"That's crazy, Vang. Boys, look here, I have orange ginger tea. I may have some black spice tea as well, but you look like root beer types. How 'bout some good old fashioned Chinese root beer imported from the American Pleasure Colony?"

"You know, General, let's live large. I'll go with the tea."

"How 'bout you, NuMing?"

"Sure, why not? I got a royal hangover. I'll go with the tea for my mental state."

"Well, you can live with your mental state all you want. Would you like some cigarettes?"

"We've never eaten those, but I think I can speak for the both of us, we really aren't hungry."

"That's too bad, 'cause I got lots of tofu too. Our tofu is a specialty of the Cangwu crater. It's a world renowned world class dish. Are you sure?"

"I'm sure, but there's always room for tofu after fifteen minutes."

"That's right, and this is the right crater for tofu. So please, help yourselves to some incense. It makes you smell good for the ladies."

"We need all the help we can get."

"Well, Vang and NuMing, we will need your help with busy work. The old proverb on the wall says: Roman hands with Russian fingers make busy work."

"Was that an ancient Multicultural Thought?"

"Nooo, it's all mine."

"Well, that was quite Random."

"So, what kind of busy work do you do?"

"We worked in a supply clerk's office. It was no gravy train. We almost lost our minds working there."

"Besides losing your mind, what did you do?"

"We mowed imitation lawns and hung posters on the bathroom walls."

"Wow, that sounds busy. Who was your boss?"

"General George Keith."

"That name sounds familiar. He must be a Big Boss."

"Sorta. After a couple of weeks, he got fed up with us and assigned us to a C.L.O.D. orbiter. He would tell us that we were an important part of an important team, and this was an important job, but we knew he just wanted to get rid of us. We worked up there a couple of years."

"What did you do on such an important ship?"

"Oh, just file papers, but mostly took inventory of crap. We had to sort, count, and classify every little piece of space junk for that hard on!"

"That is most tedious work for you."

"It was like being in a hardware store, with thousands of bins, containing little odd-shaped pieces of asteroid metal. We had to check them off, label each one, wrap it in plastic bubble wrap, put it in a lead envelope, lick the glue strip, and send it down in a shuttle pod. The junk was recycled into parts and stuff for the perpetual war effort against you. After a while, we just blew that off. We were so bored that we started practicing daily Tai Chi."

"You were becoming very good Chinese with Tai Chi. It centers you. I practice Tai Chi too. You must show me your poses. I'm not good all day unless I part the wild horse's mane."

"Yeah, I can't get off without adjusting my antenna, either."

"Numing, you are really a piece of work, you know. I want to hear more about your boring C.L.O.D. orbiter ship."

"Well, it seemed like every time we were in the middle of Tai Chi, our Puter would interrupt us with busy work crap."

"I hate when that happens!"

"All the vending machines stopped working, and we couldn't get anything to eat."

"I bet you were hungry boys."

"We remembered an old Star Trek movie, and we accidentally sorta flushed our new ship out to space because it was blocking the air vents. We couldn't have ice cream."

"Oh, I like that too."

"The ship was regenerating itself. Who knew?"

"Who knew!"

"This caused our main ship to shut down, bookoo. We couldn't live there anymore and we couldn't bring our really cool collector toys with us. It was a bummer scene, Man."

"A royal bummer!"

"We had to make it to the Escape Pods, pronto. We hit a gnarly time warp, and General George Keith sent us back to Earth in the past. Nobody believed we were from the future."

"That was a cold thing for them to do."

"Unfortunately, the slag pile we flushed out into space also, accidentally, destroyed a Chinese satellite."

"So, you were the ones!"

"Yep. It was purely Random, sir."

"But a most fortunate Random one for you."

"How's that, General Tso's Keef?"

"We are not too keen on rock music from America. We just don't get it. But that ancient satellite was lousy, bringing much static and white noise into our new television shows. We couldn't get a clear picture from that piece of junk spinning around up there. And we couldn't afford to bring it down ourselves, so you did us a big favor."

"We did?"

"Yeah, boy. It crashed not too far from here, and landed on your side of the red line. Randomly for us, it also landed on a fleet of your military rovers coming across the border. We smiled greatly watching your army pick it all up. They were bored doing busy work. Many tried to talk to us because we're friendly and have good reception now. That was a very big day for the Chinese."

"Why was that, sir?"

"It was the first time we felt popular."

"Didn't you see it as an act of war?"

"Nah. You saved us lots of money to build a new satellite. We hate to clean up anything old. You have to bury it *somewhere*. Then, someone has to dig it up, dig another hole, and put it somewhere else. It never ends."

"So, General Tso's Keef, what do you do around here?"

"I supervise all the ditch digging, rock painting, and monitor the red line. It shifts a lot in the sand. So, we're always gaining new territory. We guard the Cangwu crater. I don't know why, but it's a very busy job, very important. Also, I am the commander of Vang and NuMing. They have to be watched constantly. They're always wandering off into the crater and picking up crap. Just the other day, I caught them blowing up rock formations with cherry bombs. By the way, do you know where they are?"

"No, not really."

"Were they here when you crossed the red line?"

"Yeah, but right now, they're riding around in our C Class rover. They said they'd be back before you got here for an important job."

"Okay, okay, enough about their important job... I used to be a Supply Clerk Officer, like your General George Keith. I got assigned here after I became a hero, like you. I got promoted with real gold medals. See that on the wall? Above that new hole? Okay now, over the green dragon picture? Those are my medals."

"You must have done something really great!"

"Yes, I did."

"What did you do?"

"Well, I kinda set off a carbon bomb. It destroyed the Clone Dome antenna on your American base."

"Amazing! You? We got blamed for that. We got sent to Earth, but it's okay. We're back now and we're loaded."

"Sorry you're loaded."

"How did you set this cookie off?"

"No big deal! While I was working in the supply clerk's office, my commander sent me out to get some ink cartridges and mailing stickers. I had to xerox a whole pile of dumb orders to hang in the bathroom."

"How many times have we had to do that?"

"I noticed that the ditch wasn't straight. A crummy old pipe was in the way."

"We hate when that happens."

"I thought some busy work had to be done. So, I fired up the solar backhoe, but it couldn't go any further. When I put my office supplies down, the backhoe cut through the pipe. I heard a weird noise like something frying in a wok. It was the chemical reaction in the supply line."

"That happens to us all the time! What can you do?"

"What can you do? It took off big time and ba-boom! Out went your Clone Dome antenna like a piece of garbage. It was like a Chinese new year celebration."

"Neat. That must have been really colorful and loud!"

"Well, without Clone Dome reception, there was a big bash on your side. A big Bash. We could see all the fires and parties from over here. Lots of clones, wandering around, way too shit-faced. They were on a mad binge. They didn't know they stumbled over the red line into our territory. A lot of them fell into the ditch. We helped them out, and offered them tea to sober up. We showed them our simple ways and taught them our ancient proverbs. I guess they wanted to stay. In fact, Vang and NuMing were such clones. They were hammered and stumbled over during the big party. They are good Chinese now. Not too bad."

"They must feel like they belong. Good for them."

"Well, good for them! The next day, the pipe was gone in the ditch. It was a very strange thing. A very strange thing."

"The pipe was strange?"

"Yes, a bunch of fossil bones were where the pipe was. I brought them back to the supply office. Everyone was amazed! I discovered a fossil bird of ancient Martian life. It was worthy to put in our Chinese, most high, Museum of Natural History."

"Wow. Most worthy! Did you get money for it?"

"Nah. They're cheap. Even the medals are imitation, but they were nice enough to name the fossil after me. See, the medals say; "General Tso's Fossil Bird of ancient Martian Life," with the discovery date, and everything. I was a hero, like you, for a while."

"That is most awesome, chef!"

"Yes, this changed the way we view life on Mars, how it evolved, and everything. A major discovery. But our scientists are so smart! They burned the fossil to carbon date it. When they were finished, all that was left was the beak. They don't know how sneaky I was. I drew, most carefully, the bird bones around the beak, of course, and put it back in the display case. Nobody has noticed it since."

"I feel very changed by this, sir. Thank you. It is most profound. To know that fossil birds once flew in the Martian air, and dragons roamed around with lucky cameras, I shall never be the same. Mars is so much more cooler now. You should get mega-medals for life, dude."

"You are most kind, younger NuMing."

"General Tso's Keef, sir, I was wondering?"

"What is that, older Vang?"

"Do you ever dream of clones? From the Edgar Cayce Institute? Trying to steal your Chinese plans? For your secret operations? I was just wondering?"

"No, but sometimes, I dream of a very pretty lady flying over me. It's a very real dream. She is nice to me. She is saying something about going to a cabin in the woods in winter. She thinks I am bored and asleep, but I'm not, when she flies over the red sands."

"I've had that same dream!"

"You know about this cabin in the woods with snow falling picture?"

"No, but it sounds pretty."

"Yes. She is a very foxy lady with her thong bikini and pink starfish..."

Surr-ruumm Waah-waaah Surr-ruumm Wah

"Wait, I think hear Vang and NuMing outside. They're back with our rover!"

"Finally! Look, aah, General Tso's Keef, you're a pretty cool dude, but ya see, we gotta a big date with Pleasure Colony girls tonight, and we gotta book out of here..."

"So, what's up, Van?"

"What's up, NuMing?"

"What's up, Numan?"

"What's up, Vang?"

"Well, we tested her out. She's real good up the crater. It's quite an adequate machine if I may say so, quite adequate..."

"You totally totaled our C Class rover! Look at all the paint scratches – there's no more doors and the seats are all ripped up."

"I wouldn't call it *that*."

"What would *you* call it, then?"

"I would call it a Bent ZW Class rover. From the front, it looks like a Z, and from the side, it looks like a W."

"Well gosh, thanks for remodeling and renaming our rover. It feels like a brand new machine!"

"No problem, dude."

"Vang and NuMing, get out of there. Vang and NuMing have to get to the Pleasure Colony before it gets too late. They can't see with the headlights dangling every which way."

"You guys used up the C 45 twin hyro-cell batteries. How can we get to the Pleasure Colony now?"

"You could make it back to the west region. You're only five kilometers away. Look, I can see the new Twin Tower antennas from here. Just point your vehicle that way."

"Will you help us pick it up and point it that way?"

"We hate to pick up anything, but I guess, this one time we could."

"Well, General Tso's Keef, I was thinking. We *did* get our Bent ZW rover back. It's totaled, but we had some good tea and you *did* give us all this fancy incense. We *could* marry the Pleasure Colony girls tomorrow I guess it all worked out."

"Yes, but not all work is productive."

"Is that an ancient Random Thought, General Tso's Keef?"

"Why yes, it is. Your rover smells good now. You are almost Chinese. The girls will like you. You go now and get married fun time."

Surr-rumm *Waaah-wah Waaah-wah*

"Looks like we're just a few kilometers away, we're almost there."

"You know Van, what really gets me? I can do without all the cameras, robot arm hood ornament, steering wheel, and even the fenders. But why did they have to break off the loudspeaker? That was the one thing that made this ride so cherry."

"Yeah, I really wanted to talk to the other rovers."

"Uh-Oh, spaghetti-O's. Of all things, the engine light came on!"

"So what?"

"We can't drive with the engine light on? It might explode! We'll have to ditch it on that rock formation. Think anyone will notice?"

"Nah, it will blend in with all the other crap around here."

"Look, we're only a half kilometer away."

"We'll have to walk."

"Geez, I hope we don't get lost."

"How can we? We're on vacation."

Chapter 7
Mars
Past

"Hey, Chairman Le Jour, is that you?"

"Aah, Van and Numan, what are you doing out here?"

"We're on vacation so we get to stay up late."

"What are you guys up to?"

"We tried *real hard* to get lost around here. I am beginning to think vacations are boring. There's nothing to do. Is there a job we can do on vacation?"

"Well, you can sort Tarot cards or shine I Ching coins at the Institute. There's always a need for rover washing at the apartments. By the way, where is your C Class rover?"

"Oh that? It's in the garbage, I mean, garage B. Yeah, it's safely parked there. Don't worry. It's kind of a hassle to start. We just use it on special occasions. In fact, we were looking for you."

"What do you want?"

"It's kinda awkward to ask - could you give us some money?"

"Yeah, we need some more money because Van wants to buy his own C Class rover."

"That sounds reasonable, but Farnsworth handles all that now. Here's his card. You should go see him."

"Wow! What is this big telescope for?"

"I've been looking at the Milky Way. Earth looks so beautiful tonight, and Mercury is in retro-grade."

"What does that mean?"

"It means, business will pick up for me soon."

"Can I look? I've never seen a telescope before."

"Geez, I don't know..."

"Chairman Le Jour? I don't see anything - just some apartment windows."

"You must have bumped it or something. Here, let me show you."

"I still can't see anything."

"The lens is on the right, try using your left eye."

"Yes! I see lots of stars, now! I didn't know there were so many. There's a ton of them. There must be mega planets floating around too."

"Didn't you ever look out the port window of the C.L.O.D. orbiter, when you were up there?"

"Yeah, but we could only look down on Mars."

"See what you've been missing all these years?"

"I guess I've never looked up at night. But now, when we're looking at the stars, I feel so small. They seem so near, but I know they're far away. It's like having a question that will never be answered. Chairman Le Jour?"

"Yes, Numan?"

"I was wondering...Why are we here?"

"Weren't you looking for me?"

"No, I *mean*, why are we *here*?"

"Well, we brought you back to Mars because we had to correct the discrepancies with the Clone Labor laws. We had to have you sign some papers that..."

"No, that's not it. *I mean, why are we here?*"

"Why are we on Mars? Well, Earth was running out and getting too crowded, so we developed enough technology to settle here and..."

"Chairman Le Jour? I think what Numan wants to ask is: What is our purpose?"

"I knew what Numan was asking all along. I tend to avoid these big Random Questions of yours."

"So you know?"

"Yeah. I guess it's time for our Random *Talk*."

"You mean where babies come from?"

"Something like that, but more of where *you* come from."

"Where we came from?"

"Sort of, but more about your purpose."

"Our purpose where we come from?"

"It's a bit abstract."

"I sorta know about abstract paintings. They were done a long time ago, and they saved the pictures online."

"That's a good place to start. Those paintings are about gestures of chance and randomness. This was something we all cared about at one time. People were interested in stories where something random would happen to someone. But now, chance is predictable, and randomness, improbable. I love riddles. Let me tell you a riddle: What gets more and more as you have less and less?"

"Oh, geez, let's see. That's a hard one. I don't know? I suppose, the answer is love?"

"Nope. The answer is clones. You see, when rock stars and movies stopped being about love, we had to create it in a different way. We made clones to love us because people stopped loving each other. When that didn't work out, we made clones into athletes, so that people would love watching them compete. When that didn't work out, clones became our work force. People loved them for their labor. I think that was after about seven generations. Now, since people don't procreate anymore, clones are made to keep us company. People are basically free to have clones do whatever they please."

"But we're not free with people. How can we be free, when we have these stupid Clone Domes?"

"Yeah, it's like having shoes that are out of fashion."

"Let's talk about that fixture for a moment. I realize that Clone Domes are awkward, but you're still free to do whatever you want. Implanting Clone Domes enabled us to check in on you. It was our way of being able to call you home for dinner, as a manner of speaking. We made too much of an investment to take the risk of clones getting lost and confused. We merely call you up when we need to. It's our way of protecting you. Don't you see?"

"So, we're like pets?"

"Oh, no. You're much more than that. You're a cliche in the machine, a stutter step, a stock character. Your aging process has slowed to a crawl. You're thirty years older than I am, yet physically, you're still in your early twenties. You have an internal self, which you've used during your Remote Dreaming missions. Your Random Thought implants allow you to speak like a real person. Ultimately, you are the expression of equilibrium in randomness. That's like being a regular person."

"I don't feel regular very often."

"We tried to correct that too. When randomness didn't go the way we wanted, we had to re-create it in other ways. The more random, the better. This is what we do at the Cayce Institute. We research and develop randomness for the industry of cloning."

"Is that why we do all those funny things over there, like make daily decisions based on a coin toss?"

"Yes, but it goes deeper than that. Chance is about choice, and randomness is about circumstance. Together, they facilitate change. This is something we highly value. Cloning had certain side effects that remained static. Each generation of clones had their own particular imperfections. That is to say, bio-engineering factors, that emerged from a variable set of possibilities, played out to their ends. We just ran out of options. We had to re-introduce new implications into the cloning process. One example, was gene manipulation. Stable gene patterns would often emerge and disrupt the random permutations we configured. Our ideal was to create hybrids – angels, as it were, but we couldn't manipulate DNA beyond it's conventional paradigm. Yet, by creating these new hybrids of life, we felt closer to God. And, we're all just waiting for God to restore chaos to our world."

"Are you saying randomness hasn't changed anything?"

"No, not really, especially within the closed perimeters of cloning. If we had endless possibilities in the lab, we could have witnessed something like chaos. We were limited in many ways – with knowledge, nature, and technology. This is why I love looking at the stars. There's order in the constellations. They never change their positions, yet there's chaos swirling around in space."

"So, what happened to our chaos?"

"We had to be rigorous, because randomness and chance are just shadows of chaos. When they appeared, we thought we could appropriate their properties because of their similarities to chaos. In the end, we were deceived by this relationship. They could not produce radical change, and yet, we couldn't discover a dynamic opposite, or third element, that we could introduce chaotically. This would have given us a unique transformational element, like lead turning into gold. Look at it this way. Imagine yourself on a train."

"That's hard, but okay."

"The mountains in the distance appear to move slower than the ground near us. Events seem to happen by chance in the landscape, but they're already present before we can observe them. Cloning became an elusive combination. We intentionally dropped instruments on the floor, mixed DNA samples together as a soup, and other tactics of chance, hoping to discover some kind of miracle combination. After a while, we saw that life, like the mountains in the distance, can't be transformed. In fact, we hoped that life would become more random, the more we engineered it, rather than the reverse."

"I guess it's predictable that we go see Farnsworth now."

"You know, I *could have* seen that one coming with my Extra-Sensory perception."

"Well, I used my Random Thought implants, that's all."

"Sure Numan, you have me there. Just walk over to the apartments and look up the number on the card."

"Well, I am glad we met up with you by chance."

"That was your decision, Van."

"Yeah, this sure is a big-old random Milky Way, Chairman Le Jour."

"Stay thirsty, my friends."

"Wait, wasn't that from a beer commercial a long time ago? Are you serious?"

"If I took anything seriously, my sorrow would never end. Well, back to my star gazing. A star in the Gemini constellation is eclipsing and I want to catch it."

"Let's go look up Farnsworth now."

"Oh, and spend all your money in one place, you'll get a lot more for it."

"Thanks, Chairman dude, we gotta get going and stash the cash. Catch ya later."

"Gee, I hope Farnsworth has the cash on hand, or we'll have to hassle with the bank."

"*Man*, they ask a lot of questions, and they make you write all that stuff out."

"I hate standing in lines! You never know where to look."

"Yeah, it's really hard to stare at people's hair."

"You could stare at the ceiling, like when you meditated."

"I can't meditate at a bank, the lights are too harsh."

"Well, we could wear big sunglasses and overcoats, and cut to the front of the line. Then, we could give the girl a note and we wouldn't have to talk to her."

"You mean, we could walk in and demand our money?"

"Sure, dude, we're loaded now. We's packing. With our vacation pay? We *should* own the whole bank by now."

"For sure. Let's go tell Farnsworth that we own it now."

"Dude, look at this place! It must be for people who are well off. Why else would they have these massive gates?"

"Don't you know? It's to keep clones like us out, but since

Farnsworth handles our mega-assets, and he lives here, we must proceed."

"I can't understand why he has all this stuff around and doesn't play with it."

"Wow, he has a glass pool, a wave slide, and even a waterfall. We could totally see under water with all the pink lights and body surf that."

"I love the orange umbrellas and deck chairs. They're quite sporty, aren't they?"

"Let's scarf down some energy bars at the vending machines."

"I'll scarf after I shred some tubes."

"The tubes will wait for me, I'm gonna check out Farnsworth's apartment."

"Catch you later, Brah."

"Let's see, Farnsworth's cube starts with a number one – one is on the ground floor, and his number is on this card. Number 1108. Yep, that's it."

ring, ring...ring, ring...ring...

"Whaa?"

"We want some money now!"

"Whaa?"

"We want some money 'cause we're on vacation."

"Whaa...Who is this?"

"Is this Mr. Farnsworth?"

"Nooo."

"Does Farnsworth live here?"

"Whaa? No, not really, wait a second, I've gotta get..."

"Where is Henry Farnsworth?"

"Aah, let me, I can't... He's. What? Anything now! Whaa?..."

"Say, your voice sounds very familiar. What's your name?"

"It's Susan, why?"

"Susan, what?"

"Susan Dix. Is this a reporter with a camera or something?"

"Wow, What a coincidence. I know a Miss Dix. She told us about filing her pens, looking at her fingers, and she answered the phone. Is that you?"

"Who? Whaa? Are you some kind of weird secret agent?"

"No, it's me, Numan. You know, the appointment yesterday. You said we were very important because Chairman Le Jour never talks to you that way."

"Numan, it's five o'clock in the morning. I've got to get up early and go to work. I need my beauty sleep."

"So you *do* work for Chairman Le Jour and you *are* beautiful."

"Thank you, Numan. Is Van out there too?"

"No, he's shredding the underwater wave machine."

"How did you get this apartment number?"

"Chairman Le Jour gave it to us, but why are *you* in Farnsworth's apartment?"

"Oh, *that*? He gave it to me when I was sad. He owned too many apartments, and he needed a place to stop by."

"Miss Dix? I like talking to you on this weird speaker and all, but do you suppose I could come in?"

"Numan, it's late. Just for a while. I guess I'm still a little pliant, O.K.? I'll leave the door opened."

"I won't stay long. I gotta royally shred some waterfalls and scarf down on some... Say, I like your little cube. It's totally radical. 'Specially all the fur and velvet stuff."

"I decorated it myself. I couldn't live with Farnsworth's plaid couches anymore, even with the lights off."

"Didn't Farnsworth get mad when you changed it?"

"Nah. He doesn't have any taste in decoration. He's not aware of it when he comes over."

"I like the way it smells in here. It reminds me of Earth roses."

"That's the only thing I kept that belonged to Fansworth. He wanted to give me red flowers for Valentine's Day, so he invented a machine, you know. I really don't know how it works. I think the air vents are connected to some kind of weird fan. It blows the fragrance of any flower I want, into the cube. Listen, I'm really tired. I went to a heavy underground party last night. I am going back to bed."

"I don't mind. I'll wait."

"Wait for what? I can still feel you standing over me. Do you have to?"

"Oh, I don't mind standing. Susan? Why aren't you wearing any clothes? Aren't you cold?"

"You got me out of bed, Silly. Say, how can you see me in the dark?"

"Clone Officer Susan taught me during our dream missions. I didn't notice it before, but you have a royally stacked body - just like hers."

"Yes, but do you like *my* body?"

"Now that you ask, it's quite lovely. You must have been a volleyball player when you were younger. I love all the constellation tattoos above your twin satellites. Your narrow waist, Venus mound, and long thin ankles, are quite a bundle. Oh, by the way, should we multiply now?"

"Only if you make me do the math."

"Should we have an explicit sex scene?"

"I don't think we need any descriptive passages here."

"But, up to now, I've only practiced on plastic girls."

"Plastic makes perfect."

"Shall I re-state the obvious?"

"I maybe promiscuous, but I'm no longer pliant."

"Well then, should we make love as they used to say?"

"Perhaps, but I'm too much of a flirt. You can try me."

"I thought if everything added up, you'd feel like it."

"I would, if seduction is added to making love. It's kinda like a riddle."

"It is?"

"What gives you the most pleasure?"

"I suppose dreams do."

"Well what if there's a place where dreams come true?"

"That's awesome!"

"Dreams come true there. And if you know Earth, it's kinda like a cross between Paris, Beirut, and Wyoming."

"Earth was so crowded and hot. Is it crowded there?"

"No, not really, but everything has meaning, even the stoplights. I smile more, laugh a lot, have fun with fashion, pop up on everything - glitter is sprinkled on top. Share your heart and joy, chase your dreams and always shine, bring on the boots and let's rock!"

"Oh geez. Let's see. That could be Chairman Le Jour's office, or the Astrology Center? or..."

"You're getting me warm now!"

"The Pleasure Colony?"

"How did you guess?"

"I don't know? I guessed the Pleasure Colony and I win!"

"You're almost there, Babe."

"That's awesome! But didn't you work as a dancer. Didn't you tell me that you kicked a miner in the head? Why did you do something like that?"

"To show off my body, Silly."

"You're really a fine piece of reproduction now!"

"I only get better with Clone Dome adjustments."

"So, what can you do at the Pleasure Colony?"

"A lot of cool things: You can hang around and flirt with people, 'cause they're on vacation and you might meet someone important. Then, you can admire all the gold statues of mermaid babies in the flower gardens. You *could* visit the underground caves, where they grow magic mushrooms and crystals. Then visit the Dinosaur Park, where they make cool plaster dinosaurs 'cause that's really scary and fun. I like going to the aquarium and the zoo the most."

"I don't know, that sounds really boring."

"Why would you say that?"

"You know, it's always the same. We never had creatures on Mars, and most of the animals on Earth are extinct or imitation; you can only see pictures of them. The only animals alive are those mangy cats, dogs, and mutant anteaters."

"But they're so cute."

"Yes, but I would've liked to pet a giraffe or a tiger, at least. As for the aquarium, the only thing alive are crazy jellyfish and sea urchins, and they don't do much."

"Maybe, but I like the imitation fish. With all their colors? And the way they painted the backgrounds. With all that detail? It's quite amazing."

"I guess now that you described it, it would be cool."

"It's quite amazing."

"So, what do the Pleasure clones do?"

"Oh, they do their laundry to smell nice. Then, they visit the tanning reactors for a glowing skin color. Then, they go to the clubs. Sometimes they dance, but usually, they just stand around waiting to be discovered."

"What do you mean?"

"Well, you know, only the Second Generations can dance. They do these really cool gymnastic moves. All the others trip over themselves 'cause they can't do the beat. They just stand around, waiting to become famous."

"But don't they all look alike?"

"No, not really, there's all colors and sizes to choose from. There are happy Pleasure girls and sad Pleasure girls. Girls who climb on rocks, buff girls, prissy girls. Even girls with polka dots. Really! All kinds - I don't know."

"Susan, what did you say about dreams coming true?"

"They have these centers. I think they call 'em salons or saloons. They have all these comfy couches, where they put you under with a sleeping vapor. No, actually, I mean, they give you a choice: Either they give you a drug, so that it's easier for you to choose your dreams, or you can let *them* manipulate your dreams if you want. It becomes very strong and vivid. They scan your awareness, and tune you into your dreams. It's kinda like a disc-jockey spinning desires into your dreams."

"That doesn't sound so great. I can already do that on my own."

"That may be, but some clones *can't*."

"Well, I *can*."

"*Dude*, some clones *can't!*"

"I can't help that!"

"*Well, dude*, some clones just can't... Oh, it's getting daylight. I gotta get going. If we argue anymore, my head's going to explode!"

"See? I should have known how these things go. I get tricked into being passive all the time! We talked all night, but that didn't get us anywhere. Why do I randomly think I could talk you into it."

"You could help me choose my bra and panties."

"Well, two out of three ain't bad."

"This lacy thing has always been a terror, but Chairman Le Jour likes it."

"Susan, it's not the straps, or the cups. It's the band. The band supports your Girls. Clone Officer Susan told me."

"Enough about her, O.K.? Do you like this outfit?"

"It's totally sleek on you. Earth green is the new Crater red - so you're in. It should be a lot shorter though."

"You're are such a flirt! I am beginning to like that!"

"You do? Maybe we should flirt all over again, but I guess at this point, we should go look for Van. I am sure he's wondering what's up."

"Oh, yeah, Van. Where is he?"

"You never know. I think he's body surfing out at the pool."

"He's sooo cute! You should have brought him along, then we could have done some *major* flirting."

"Well, I did the math and one can't be divided by two."

"Numan, do I hear some jealousy in your voice? That really turns me on."

"Dang it! I should have Randomly known."

"Look, there's Van, but he's with a girl. Now I won't get a chance to flirt with the both of you..."

"Hey Van! Who's the neat girl by the pool?"

"Oh, she's an Earth girl. She's watching me body surf."

"Hi, my name's Sharon. You must be Numan and Susan. Van told me about you guys coming along. So, I've been watching him swim *and* reading my book."

"Cool. What's the book about?"

"Oh, it's about these two goofy clones who go on vacation, get captured by the Chinese, and get their rad rover ripped off. I haven't finished the rest."

"Do you enjoy reading this book?"

"Perhaps, maybe, or unsure."

"Do you think the author's from the future?"

"Perhaps, maybe, or unsure."

"That reminds me of a funny joke: What happens when a *General* goes on vacation?"

"I don't know...What?"

"His shuttle hits some of *our* uncollected space debris and sends him permanently off to Titan. Ha-ha, get it?"

"No, not really. It must be an inside joke."

"It *is* an inside joke."

"What do you do, Sharon?"

"Not much. There's not much to do anymore. I just travel around, doing leisure."

"What's leisure?"

"Leisure is about experiencing things, expanding your mind by thinking, and personal reflection. Reading is done during leisure. You have time for things like that."

"That sounds important."

"It is important. Our lives are short. We need time to think about life. If we're always doing something for someone else, we're distracted from creating our own lives, pursuing our own interests, desires, or even making cool things – like jewelry. You grow as a person if you have leisure. Van told me that you're on vacation. That's a type of leisure, but it sounds like you're not using your time well."

"Well, what should we do?"

"Actually, I'm on my way to an underground night club called the Red Sun's Zenith. It's a really cool place to hang out and do leisure. We should go there."

"I don't know. Susan? Don't you have to go to work today?"

"Heck no. Not after all that. I need to get some leisure, right now. Let's go! My rover is parked out front by the gates. I'll drive."

"But don't you? Won't Chairman Le Jour get mad?"

"He doesn't know I'm there half the time. Besides, he's attending seminars in Advanced Rorschach Ink Blot painting this week. He never checks his messages. Let's get going. I want to get in some leisure, pronto."

"Everyone climb aboard."

"Look Van, we's double dating!"

"Yeah, we's styling, and we don't even have to drive."

"O.K. Set your rover's co-ordinances for the Red Sun's Zenith in the Gale crater. I hope your Puter is better than our R Puter. That thing was a mess."

"Wasn't the Gale crater famous for something? I've always been curious about that area."

"Maybe we'll get curious when we get there."

"Looks like a good day to go for a drive with the solar windows down."

"Maybe, we'll see some Chinese army men we can flirt with."

"Will you stop *that*."

"Does this thing have a loudspeaker on top?"

"Leave that shifter alone, Numan. If you're gonna sit in front, you better kick back."

"Can we, at least, put on some wild tunes?"

"I love all the glitter stickers and pink fur in your rover, Susan. It matches my purse: Moon Pink is the new Cheese Green, you know."

"Gee, thanks, Sharon. I decorated it to match my apartment."

"Well, it's really Posh and Now."

"I really try to be in. Oh, Van? Would you check my fuel cell, battery level?"

"How do I do that, Susan?"

"Just look in my dial on my dash board, honey."

"Don't you have a Puter to do that?"

"I'd rather have you look. It's right between the seats, dear."

"I can see it's fully charged."

"Then I'm ready to go, if you are?"

"Oh, I am willing and able, sugar girl."

"My motor's running now. Let's get to it..."

"If I may cut in between you two for a moment."

"I don't mind, Sharon."

"In all my days of leisure traveling, there's just one thing I hate."

"What's that?"

"I hate all the trash and rubbish left in the landscape. There's trash everywhere. For example, look at that piece of shit on that rock formation over there."

"Hey, that's our ZW rover!"

"How did it get there?"

"Well, we tried to get lost. We had some incense and some heavy root beer. We didn't know how to paint a red line, but the engine light came on and we were scared, so we ditched it."

"You should have more pride in Mars, and take the trash out. There's trash everywhere here. I hate trash 'cause trash is trash. Once it's trash, it's always trash. People should never throw it away, on the ground, that is, 'cause it looks like trash. We should go to Alaska where it's clean. There's no trash there. Everyone there knows how to throw trash away."

"Say, Sharon? You look quite familiar."

"I should. A long time ago, some weird computer on Earth, used my mother's DNA to create a bunch of Clone Officers. There's bits and pieces of her DNA scattered in First Generation clones all over Mars. Even I get confused when I meet them."

"How did that happen?"

"Well, she was a just a typical Earth girl, living near the ocean. One night, while she was at a beach party, she saw something strange."

"What was that?"

"A blue light fell from the sky over the ocean. A shiny nautilus floated to shore, dissolving like paper, around twin boys who swam in the rest of the way. They walked up to the fire ring and joined the party. Everyone was so amazed to hear their tales of Mars, that they gave them food, clothes, and a place to live. But these wondrous twins turned out to be real beach bums. They played in the sand all day, collecting seaweed, glass, and shells. At times, they lived under the pier and slept on old ratty blankets that they found. All the young surfer girls would follow them along the boardwalk. They couldn't get a job, so all they did was meditate and drink beer. They totally trashed her apartment and burned the furniture.

Yet, all the while, claimed to be rock stars from Mars, which no one really believed at the time."

"Why didn't they believe them?"

"Well, back then, nobody lived on Mars, and they said they were from the future. How could anyone believe that? But look at what happened recently: We're from the future now. People live on Mars. That didn't happen so long ago."

"Yeah, that's right. We're from the future now!"

"Hey, 'member how they thought the world would end back in 2012, with that weird calendar?"

"Dude? The world *did* end."

"Not then. We just ran out of shit and that was that, who would've known?"

"Who would've known?"

"So anyway, what happened?"

"One day, she showed the boys a computer-like thingy near the tide pool. The machine tricked her into licking an apple, which gave it a sample of her DNA. Not long after that, the boys left in a space ship."

"How did she know it was a space ship?"

"Well, if you saw a weird octahedral shaped thingy, that looked like a big red Christmas ornament, parked outside of a taco stand, wouldn't you think it was from the future?"

"It sounds like one of those blow-up advertisement they used to do."

"I think they shouldn't have left that way. That was sad."

"It was. Even though the boys looked like twins, she fell in love with both of them. Her heart was conflicted. She knew that one day she would have to choose one over the other. This made her decision even more difficult. They were so poor, they didn't care if they had anything. It was as though they never took care of themselves. She was the only one who loved them and looked after them. She even did their laundry. Because of that, she lost all of her friends. This didn't matter to her – what mattered was that they were taken away on the day she would have made her decision."

"So after these boys left in the Christmas ornament, what happen to her?"

"She was lonely for a long time and never forgot her first love. She went to college to study economics like a typical Earth girl. She went on to become a Professor of Space Debris Recycling. Then, she met a Mathematics Professor, who shared the same interests. They fell in love and had me."

"That sounds like everything turned out all right."

"Sort of. My dad was so excited by the idea of a Mars Colony from the future, that when the opportunity came, he left her and I, and came up here. He was one of the first men, along with Chairman Le Jour, who established the Edgar Cayce Institute for Research and Development. When I finished my studies in early 20th century French poetry, I flew up to join him."

"So, your father knows Chairman Le Jour?"

"Yeah, they're good friends. They met at a seminar for Sleep-Inducing, Random Hermetic Theory."

"What's his name?"

"Phillip."

"Phillip, what?"

"Phillip Das Nacht."

"Is your dad Chairman Das Nacht?"

"Yep, that's my daddy."

"Wow, everyone talks about him, but no one has really seen him. I think I've seen him only once, from a distance. He was passing by in the courtyard. Susan? Have you ever seen Chairman Das Nacht in Chairman Le Jour's office?"

"I don't know. Lots of random people come and go to flirt in that office. I am not sure who he is or what he looks like."

"Well, I think my daddy is a very elegant man. He's intriguing and quite formidable. Everyone thinks he's mysterious because he works behind the scenes. No one sees him because he's so entranced with his work. Yet, he always has time for me. He calls me his "Headlight Child." I'll always be his baby doll girl."

"Sharon? You're a real people person, you know that?"

"Well, I would like to meet your daddy one day. I think my Generation is too old to have anything in common with your mom."

"I am curious too. If he's like Chairman Le Jour, he's probably really awesome."

"Yes, he's very influential. You'll meet him - he owns the Red Sun's Zenith."

"We've just pass the outskirts of the Gale crater. The Red Sun's Zenith is at the center."

"All right! We're going to find leisure now."

"Susan? Put me on your rover's loudspeaker: *Hey all you mofo clones! We's on vacation, we's loaded, and we're here to par-taay!*"

Chapter 8
The Red Sun's Zenith Club Present

"Welcome to da Zenith, ladies."

"Oh-la, Mister Bouncer. We's double dating!"

"Ho-ho-he! Dese fine ladies can't be with youse guys."

"For sure, buff dude. These are our dates. So, part thy waves and let us proceed, pronto."

"Wait a minute. Are youse da dorks who pulled up in dat swishy pink rover? I would never!"

"Yep, my date can drive! Can she not?"

"Youse gotta be kiddin' me."

"No way, dude, we's loaded."

"My flash on youse is, if youse packin', youse better be loaded."

"Oh, we's packin' all right."

"Do youse fine ladies really go with dese doofuses?"

"Well, I'm promiscuous and she watched him body surf."

"Well, or-din-narrowly, I woulda let dese two lovely ladies pass without youse guys, but since da're classy, and one is a real Earth girl, I'll let it slide dis time. If I were youse guys, I wouldn't come alone to da

Zenith."

"Why is that, Bouncer Dude?"

"'Cause, between youse and me, I've whacked guys for less."

"Less than what?"

"Less than... Hey, dat's kooky. Youse guys must be from da funny papers."

"I know you are, but what am I?"

"Aaa, don't push it, wise guy. Now, who's gonna pony up?"

"My daddy has an office here, so we get in free."

"Dis lady has some balls! I kinda respect dat."

"That's okay, Sharon. I got a roll of tens from Farnsworth. Let me get this."

"Hey Dorkus! Youse better cough it up. If youse would've let dat lady pay, I shall gladly wipe da floor with your face!"

"Geez, man! Don't have a cow. Here's your stupid money. O.K.?"

"He-he, youse guys made my night! I haven't seen grease-ball cashola since I worked at da bowling ally. I'm so glad I can make change now, ha-ha. Youse can proceed, *Ladies*. Don't let da door hit youse in the ass."

"The nerve of that guy! I'm going tell my daddy that *you* want him fired. Then we'll see who's boss."

"That's O.K., Sharon. Let it go, okay? He was kinda polite. He's probably having a bad day. These Eleventh Generation guys don't bother me."

"Well, someone needs to stand up to that de-evolved goon. Just say the word, I'll tell my daddy, and he'll make that bully apologize to you for his rudeness."

"No, no, don't do that. He would probably cry like a big baby. I don't want to hurt his feelings."

"Didn't he put you down? We need to put jerks like him in his place."

"That's okay, forget about it. Let him stand alone outside with the crowd."

"Wow, the Red Sun's Zenith is everything I thought it would be."

"It looks bigger in here than it did from the outside. It's not so dumpy!"

"Why did they paint everything black – they might as well paint it all one color."

"The gold statues of Rock Stars look so real! They even put their pants in cool picture frames."

"This place is living large. We're sure to find leisure Pleasure girls now."

"Yeah, look! Some are dancing in furry cages."

"That matches my pink rover! Maybe they'll think I'm famous!"

"Are we all together? I can't see in these flashing lights."

"Sharon is already out on the dance floor."

"Hey Numan? Everybody's younger than us. We must be the only Seventh Generation clones here. We're gonna get slammed."

"I really peel stout of lace in he's unicorns!"

"What? I can't hear you. Holler in my ear!"

"I really feel out of place in these uniforms!"

"You silly kneel out of case in dese you-need-dorms?"

"Whaaat?"

"This club is scary 'cause the music is so loud!"

"His love is hairy does the music's slow proud?"

"One two free four. Boom, crashing cymbal, wah-wah. "Kick it. Oh, baby,

*kick it over there. Whoa, kick it! Kick it like you've never done before."
Hysterical screaming with a rush of very loud indeterminate random sounds and feedback, pulse, pulse, pulse..."*

"That srong sounds Mary from-ill-your?"

"Whaaat?"

"That song sounds very familiar!"

"Hey, Susan?! Van and me wrote this song, but this Janitor ripped us off."

"You and Dan roped this wrong, but his nan-it-tour tipped you cough?"

"Oh, forget it! Do you want something to eat? The food looks good!"

"Yeah! I link the mood lucks grood."

"Numan? Someone is squeezing my hand, I'm afraid to look."

"You'll have to holler in my ear, Van."

"Look at who's squeezing my hand, I am afraid to look!"

"Oh, it's just Sharon. She wants you to buy her a drink or a new dress. Ask her."

"Hey Sharon! Do you want me to buy you a new dress?"

"Sure, I'll tell you when I take off my new dress. I've watched you long enough. Let's go to my place and fool around."

"You want to coal to your lace and pool a sound? It's – aah, I really can't hear you."

"I can hear you fine."

"You think I am fine?"

"Yeah babe, I really do. Let's go."

"Numan? We'll catch you and Susan later. Sharon wants me to glow at her lace and pool the sound."

"Go her place and fool around? Hey dude, go for it. We'll stay and get discovered."

"Come on, Van. I don't have all night."

"Where's this lace and pool sound?"

"There's no lace and pool, Silly. We're going to my *place* so we can *fool* around."

"I'm glad to get out of there. My ears are still ringing. Where are we going?"

"My cube is real close, just through these gardens, down this walkway."

"This is a really posh place!"

"Yep, pure luxury. Just one of a few places my dad set up for me."

"This triple cube is totally boss! It's got bookoo curtains, indoor carpets, and a patio. It's everything Neo-Martian!"

"It came that way. I didn't have to hassle with any decorations."

"Well, they have impeccable taste. I've never seen such opulence. I could really live here."

"All my supplies are delivered automatically. I just check off what I want."

"Geez, you must be well off."

"I guess you could say so. Having a daddy like mine has its rewards. I never think about it. It's just the way life is."

"Well, you've really got some high class leisure here."

"Let me throw a few more pillows on the floor. The solar fire pit will start up in a moment. Help yourself to any food or wine on the counter. It's imported from all over. I really don't care where it's from, it all tastes good."

"Where are you going, Sharon?"

"To the bathroom."

"Why are you going to the bathroom?"

"I'm going to the bathroom, Silly. Sometimes I wonder about you... Van? I'm getting in the shower now. You can come in, you know."

"Really? Wow! I love all the painted tile. It's so clean. This shower must have at least fifty settings. I, personally, love the typhoon setting."

"Come in with me, honey. Don't be shy. There's lots of robes and towels for you."

"I suppose you have all the essential oils and lotions too?"

"Yeah, they're in the cabinet. Help yourself. Oh, throw me that bottle of shampoo."

"You'll never run out of this stuff."

"Everything's imported from the Pleasure Colony. I get to try them out before the Pleasure girls get to. Take some, I can't leave the door opened too long with the summer rain setting."

"You have a royally stacked body – for an Earth girl. Your thin waist gives it all away to your thighs, and this shampoo makes your hair smell like candy surf board wax. It's quite a bundle."

"Should we have an explicit shower scene now?"

"I already went swimming. So, can I watch you this time?"

"Sure, but I have a few lady things to do, if you don't mind."

"Not at all. Up to now, I've only practiced on plastic girls."

"Practice makes perfect!"

"Shall I be ambiguous then?"

"Only if you admire the obvious."

"Well then, should we flirt, as they used to say?"

"I think we've passed that point, sweetheart."

"So there's no need for seduction?"

"Not really. I'll be out soon, and then we'll go at it! Oh, by the way, could you be a dear and do a few things for me?"

"Sure, I'll do anything for you."

"Would you change the light bulb in the kitchen, straighten the picture frame in the hall, wash the dishes, vacuum the rug, water the orchid by the door, and take the trash out?"

"Don't you have a robot maid to do all that?"

"Nah, this cube doesn't have *everything*. My Daddy tries so hard. He always comes so close, so close. I guess he doesn't want to spoil me. I still have to do *some* things."

"Maybe you should have someone be a robot maid?"

"I need a real boyfriend to do that."

"Is that why you're asking me?"

"Aah, sure, why, yes, it is. I thought if everything added up, you'd do it. Are you mad at me?"

"No, but it's confusing, like a riddle."

"Well, there's no mystery about it."

"So, I'll be like a real robot maid, then?"

"It would give me pleasure if you'd do it, okay? Hurry up now..."

"... Alright. Sharon? I did it. What did you want me to do after I straighten the picture frame?"

"Wash the dishes, Dear."

"... Sharon? You still in the shower?"

"Yes, honey. Is there a problem?"

"Nooo. I did the vacuum. It kinda sucked a few things up – you'll have to look. But, what did you want me to do after I watered the dishes?"

"Just the trash, Dear! Just take out the trash and I'll be finished waxing in here."

"Okay. Be right back..."

ring, ring...

"Sharon. Sharon?"

ring, ring...

"Come on, Sharon?! I took the trash out, **Shaaronn?!**"

ring, ring...

"**Shar!...**"

"Hey, Van! What are you doing? Everybody can hear you!"

"Hey, Numan. Hi Susan. I was solving this riddle while doing this stuff and Sharon can't come to the door."

"Are you sure this is her door?"

"Yeah, brah. It's got all her constellations on it. I remembered it when I went in."

"Dude? Everybody's looking. Let's get out of here."

"But Sharon promised we'd fool around after I did all this..."

"Hey bro, 'member? She's an *Earth* girl. They want everything all the time. All the time. Let's go back to the club, dude."

"Alright. I was getting real tired of doing all this confusing work crap anyway. Besides, Sharon reminds me of Susan."

"She reminds you of *Susan*?"

"No way, dude. She reminds me of *Typical Earth girl Susan*. 'Member? We had nothing in common with her."

"Oh, that girl. She came over and cleaned our apartment. You did confusing stuff like that for *her*?"

"Yeah, it was like I was reminded of what she did for us, only I had to do it for her in a certain weird order."

"That's crazy. How did you keep track of all that?"

"I couldn't. I just skipped the things I couldn't remember.

Straightening the picture frame was a royal bitch! Could you handle doing that?"

"No way. We had a hard time just taping the signs on the wall, when we worked for the supply office. We almost lost our minds trying to do that. I can see why you dumped her."

"Can we go see the fortune teller now? Can we go see the fortune teller now? I wanna go see the fortune teller!"

"Susan, take it easy. Van got locked out, maybe he doesn't want to go."

"Sure, Numan, I'll go. Maybe she'll tell me that it worked out as a future robot maid. I really could have gone for living large there – I'd show *her* a few things to check off."

"This pin-striped tent is weird. It's got green hearts, blue moons, purple stars, and orange clovers. They're all my lucky charms!"

"Yaaay! It's the fortune teller's tent. She must love us!"

"So, Susan? What are you going to find out from this fortune teller?"

"I don't know? Her name is Madame Bardon. She's very famous. Maybe we'll be famous too. She can see what will happen."

"Why do you want to know what will happen? Won't it happen away?"

"Not really, 'cause I'll be able to change what happens before it does."

"But what if you like what she says?"

"Then I won't change anything. I'll be happy when it happens."

"What if you think it will happen and it doesn't?"

"Then I really didn't know what will happen."

"But you already knew. Won't you'll be disappointed?"

"No, I'll remember and forget it later."

"How can you do that?"

"I'll use my Random Thought implants to make it seem more random. Then I won't be surprised when it happens."

"You are so hot!"

"Who's going in first?"

"I don't know? Let's all go in together."

ring... a... ding... ding..

"Surprise! We want to know the future!"

"Vould you all mine vaiting outzide vor a little vile?"

"Sure, no problem, we'll go, sorry, Madame. We didn't mean to..."

"Oh, my god. Oh, my god! Did you see that?"

"What?"

"That old sea-hag in there with all those stuffed animals?"

"No way, Brah. She was the most gorgeous woman I've ever seen! She was a blonde sex bomb, totally. You never see women like that, alone, or in public. Ever!"

"Susan? Van and I have this argument. What did you see in there?"

"I just saw a red-headed lady in a black dress with a purple scarf. She was young, nice, but very plain Earthy looking. Oh, there were lots of candles in there, too."

"That means... We all saw something different. I am totally freaking out."

"Yeah, I am too scared to go back in there."

"Well, she didn't bother me."

"Okay, Susan. You go in there with her. Van and I will stay out here."

"You guys are scaredy cats."

"I don't care. That lady is totally whacked!"

"Well, she's gonna tell me my fortune. I'll know what will happen, and you'll miss out on what's happening."

ring... a... ding... ding..

"You may henter on your hown free vill."

"Hi there, Miss Madame. Aah, Miss Bardon?"

"Vhy, yesss, dearie. Ahren't you a sveet young zhing. Vot is your name?"

"Miss Dix."

"Oh, dat's a good von! Or do you have troubal remembering two?"

"Hey! The other is Susan. Say, what's with the accent?"

"I don't khave any aczent. You never know, zhey could be typos?"

"Are you a witch, or something?"

"No, my dear. I'm merely a scholar."

"Well then, what are your credentials?"

"You mean my qualifications?"

"Yeah, your qualifying credentials!"

"Vell, I am quite a backseat driver. I'm distantly related to Franz you-know-who. I teach Sleepwalking classes at the community college. I went to Siberia and fell in love with a Tibetan Monk. Then, I got my bell rung using ayahuasca with an Urarina shaman. I also do a lot of GOP campaign advising on the side. Doesn't that qualify me as a fortune teller?"

"Well, I guess so, but that stuffed moose is kinda weird. It looks like a cartoon or something."

"*V*ell th*A*n, let *M*e *P*roceed. Vhat v*I*ll you vant, Ta*R*ot cards or th*E* Crystal ball? I can do speculations too?"

"I want you to read my palm, please."

"Oh, we can do that. Now, place your palms down on the table, slowly turn them over and bring them up to me. Let me see here... Are you kidding me?!"

"Whaaat?"

"You don't have any creases on your hands, honey. They're as smooth as glass."

"I know."

"Then why did you tattoo lines on them?"

"I wanted to have my palms read."

"My dear child, it will always be the same, no matter who reads them. These lines are copied from a palm reading chart. You'll get the same reading every time. Okay? Well now, we *could* use a different technique of fortune telling. I can scan your irises and read the flecks in them. This will tell me your destiny. But, as I examine you, I can see that your irises are a completely solid color... You are a Seventh Generation clone, my dear!"

"Well, *dah!* I could have told you that!"

"I guess this eliminates the option of reading the bumps on your head or analyzing your hand writing."

"Can't you tell me anything?"

"Not much at this point. I left part of my tarot card deck in my classroom. So, that's out."

"Don't you have any love potions we can fool around with?"

"Nah, none of them taste any good. Take a vitamin instead."

"You know, Madame Bardon, with all these candles, lucky charms, and stuffed animals, I thought you'd be playing with half a deck. O.K., I'll give you one last chance. I paid good money to get in here."

"So you want to do the crystal ball? That's always a good one."

"I guess so, but please try. I want to know what will happen. 'K?"

"I'll have to lower the lights to warm up the magic crystal."

"This is getting spooky, Madame."

"Okaay. Let's see now. As I gaze into my crystal ball... I see... *your face*. Would you mind sitting back and not lean in too close? I'm the only one permitted to look into the future. Let's see now..."

"Will I meet a handsome stranger?"

"You'll always meet strangers, but I suppose, you'll meet someone like that."

"Will I go on a long journey?"

"I think you might, but I have a feeling it will be interrupted."

"Interrupted?"

"You could stay or you could go."

"Will I be happy?"

"I suppose you could, it all depends."

"All depends on what?"

"Whether you like it or not."

"Will I be successful at my career?"

"What do you do now?"

"I am a receptionist."

"Do you like doing that?"

"I guess so. I get to flirt with a lot of people."

"Then the crystal ball tells me... Yes! Your flirting will take you far in your career."

"Oh, goody! I knew I was gonna win the typing contest this year."

"How many words per minute can you type, my dear?"

"About ten easy words, if it's a good day."

"Then, I see that the contest will be on a good day."

"Alright! So, all I have to do is show up, and I'll win?"

"Okay, that's it. That's your limit of questions for today."

"Can't you do a few more tiny ones? Read the bottoms of my feet. I'll slip my shoes off?"

"Nah, something tells me they're a lot like your palms."

"How 'bout reading my body odor? I heard doctors can tell a lot from a person's sweat."

"Yuck! No way. I am a scholar, not a scientist!"

"How about looking in my ears? Can't you read ear wax?"

"No. Not today, your Clone Dome will interfere."

"But I'm having so much fun! This is so cool."

"We're done, sweetheart. Why don't you bring in those two young men? I can take two at a time. Let them have a chance."

"So the four of us could do some major flirting?"

"Perhaps. They looked like nice boys who know what's happening."

"Oh, they're clueless. You freaked them out. They're scared of you-know-who."

"Hey. *L*ook, I'm not *A*ll bad. I jus vant so*M*e bod*I*es like your p*A*ls out there. But if you don't feel like it, that's alright. I can cook up something in the mean time. So, help yourself to some candy. It's my way of showing good customer relations."

"Thanks, Madame. At least, I get *something* out of this..."

"Is that General George Keith over there?"

"Gee, I don't know, Numan. He's not wearing a uniform. He's all dressed up in some crazy clothes, but I sorta recognize his stupid freckled face."

"Let's go over and hassle him."

"Okay, but I think we should wait for Susan. She's been in there a while now. She might be scared what will happen. That lady was a freak-a-do."

"So, what if that really is his Generalship?"

"Then we shall give him some royal shit for not being at his post for a change."

"Oh, there's Susan. My foxy date!"

"What's up, Numan? What's up, Van?"

"What are you eating?"

"I don't know? Some icky candy corn I guess. It *was* like Halloween in there."

"You look like you got told."

"Nah. She was like every other fortune teller."

"How's that?"

"I was having fun. She said the same thing every fortune teller has, except that I'll win the typing contest this year, but I already knew that."

"Are you gonna use your Random Thought implants to forget about it?"

"Yeah. This time, *I'll* just sit there and file *my* nails."

"Susan? Van and I think we saw General George Keith. We want to go over there and give him some shit."

"Why? Wasn't he confused all the time? Wasn't he a royal doofus?"

"But he was our General Dude."

"He loves us!"

"He's at that black jack table. Let's pretend nothing's happened and give him the royal business. He won't know what's going on."

"Hmm, hmm. So, uh, deal us in, dude. Hmm, hmm!"

"Like Wow, Man! My old pals, Van and Numan."

"Oh-la, General Kiethmeister Keister. Long time, no see."

"Who is this girl? She's a real honey pot! What's your name,

Sweetheart?"

"This is Susan, so keep your hands off the merchandise, Dude!"

"Well, Susan, you're a living doll. I could eat you up!"

"Ah, General? So, what happened to..."

"Not now, kids. I wanna take this sweet young thing out and watch her try on some high-heeled shoes with silk stockings. Would you like that, Honey?"

"Stand back, General. She's already kicked a miner in the head."

"Is he flirting with me?"

"Get a grip on it, sir. Weren't you on permanent vacation?"

"Oh, that? Wow! I got my kicks during that trip."

"How's that?"

"I bummed around on Titan and got caught up into some weird shit. I shacked up with a lady who lived in a bus, but after a while, she kept bugging me to buy her a trailer. So, I went underground where people are into poetry. I couldn't understand half of what they talked about, half the time. Talk about disorder, I almost lost half my mind with half of those people. They bored me with all their political crap, their heavy drug use, and alternative farming. Really. Picking lettuce under ultraviolet lights, making imitation banana nut bread, and wearing socks with Earth shoes is not my cup of tea. So, I hitched a ride back to Mars and go lost again. They painted my office and changed my desk around. I didn't know where I was! I was AWOL by that time, so I got out, but civilian life is tough. I didn't know what to do."

"Didn't you lose all your retirement benefits and rank?"

"My bennies and my hash marks? That's alright, man. I am a first class dealer now. Everything's cool, man. I'm in real tight with Chairman Das Nacht. He bought me a righteous pad. You and Susan, will have to come over, for aperitifs. By the way, how did *you* get a doll face like Susan?"

"Well, she's promiscuous and curious – she came along to find out what's happening."

"You've got to be kidding me? I'd liked to know what's happening with her."

"She's got issues, sir. That girl is complicated."

"I can dig that scene. So, what are you cool people up to, Man?"

"We're loaded and we're on vacation. We came here with Sharon to find leisure."

"Sharon Das Nacht? Hey Man, you'd better cool it with her. People think the Chairman is the Man, but she's the one who really pulls the strings around here."

"She already pulled it with Van. I guess he couldn't qualify as a robot maid."

"That's wild, man. That's crazy. So, uh, what tunes are you guys into?"

"We really like "Kick it!" by Master Janitor Rico."

"That's tight! They play that a lot around here. It's very popular with the Fifth Generation. I am gonna go download that number right away."

"Oh, yeah? Rico ripped us off."

"Oooh, snap! Now I get the scene, Man! That was when I sent him up there 'cause we were behind. He got freaked out by some weird voice and split from the ship. Everyone thinks he's a genius that got too high and went insane. Rico is a real cult figure now. He's a kooky dude. He's off the charts. He went to live with his sister on Earth, but nobody really knows what happened to him."

"I guess we never could have sued him, if he was far out like that."

"Hey, Man, where did you guys get those neat threads?"

"Our what?"

"You know, those cool clothes?"

"These grubby things? They are basic issued C.L.O.D. orbiter uniforms. Don't you remember?"

"I didn't know they were so in!"

"Well, they're all worn out. I've got holes in my knees. We're not dressed like everybody else."

"That look sets you apart, totally, man. Everyone's looking and wants to know where to get that gear of yours!"

"Standard issue, like I said."

"Cool! So, who does your hair? It looks so freakin' happening!"

"I guess, we do. We really don't do *anything*."

"See?... That's the way things are today, man. Nobody does anything and it becomes the latest. That's how I want to be."

"General? I was wondering?"

"Hey, call me Keister. I like that."

"Okay, Mister Keister. You seem so different now. How did you get so...?"

"My swag? I got turned on by Chairman Das Nacht. He can read your thoughts, you know. He saw how confused I was and put me through some heavy shit, man. Real dream analysis with sleep altering drugs. He read my mind that I didn't have to join, lead, or follow, anymore. Just accept myself for who I was. I changed my dreams with his help. Although, I still have the need to order people around, or re-enact a few battle scenes. I can't help it, I am so lonely."

"Speaking of Chairman Das Nacht, have you seen him around

here?"

"Sure. He's sitting right next to you."

"Chairman Das Nacht? Excuse me. I never would've known. My name is Van, this is Numan, and this is..."

"I'm well aware of who you all are. In fact, I've been waiting for you."

"You have? Well then, let's all play some black jack. Deal us in Keister Meister!"

"Yeah, dude, I got a whole roll of tens burning in my pocket. I'll cover for all of us."

"Two cards each? Okay. I got clubs and spades!"

"I've got clubs and spades, too. I win."

"Wait, how do we bet on this?"

"You bet on the numbers – 21 and under."

"Not on the black?"

"That's a different game, Susan."

"Would everyone like a drink? It's on me. I own the club."

"Sure, let's go for it - if everything adds up?"

"Black Russians, all around, for my friends, here. I'm full, so espresso, black, for me."

"What's in this? It's kinda foamy."

"That's vodka and black coffee liqueur."

"Well, this is a high class drink!"

"Hey Numan? Why does it say "Leave Now!" at the bottom of my glass?"

"I don't know, Van? It could be a forewarning or something."

"Aaa-hmm, aaa-hmm!"

"Chairman Das Nacht? You don't look so good. Are you all right?"

"I am fine. Listen, I've been wanting to meet you for a long time. I would have set up a meeting, but my astrological chart said it wasn't the right time. I know you've been with my daughter. That's alright with me, but things are changing. I need a replacement. I'll make an offer for you. What would you say if you could have all of this?"

"The Red Sun's Zenith? That's awesome!"

"Yes, and more."

"Cool. I'd paint it a different color, though."

"I'd make sure all the waitress flirt the correct way."

"I'd make sure all the Puters mix the newest cocktails."

"I had a feeling you'd be into the idea. Let's all make a move to my office and work out the details, shall we?"

"Sure, we's on vacation, and we's gonna book an offer now!"

Chapter 9
Chairman Das Nacht's Office
Future

"You really have a posh office, Chairman Das Nacht."

"Yeah, even the black leather couches aren't covered in plastic."

"So, we're ready to work out the deal when you are."

"Susan, Van, and Numan? Your vacation is over!"

"You *dick*!"

"No way, Chairman Das Dude. We belong to Chairman Le Jour."

"You'll all go on a mission for me. That's *it!*"

"No, no, that's okay. Chairman Le Jour has always been nice to us. He bought us a new Bent ZW rover and handles all our assets. He owns us. I think you'll need permission from him."

"Okay. We'll call him then, and see what he says."

"Knock yourself out, dude."

"Yeah, he'll tell you a thing or two."

"Roi? Phillip, here. Yes. Yes. Yeah, I'll be there. What? My tarot card design won the Most Artistic? Wonderful! We'll have to celebrate at the Zenith. Saaay, Can I borrow Susan, Van, and Numan, for a while? Yeah? It's for a little mission I have in mind. Yes? My assistant Toby? Oh, he met with a most unfortunate accident and is unable to meet the requirements. Yeah. That's why I could use 'em. So, are you on board for that? *Okay.* Thanks plenty. Yeah, I'll see you at the office tomorrow, Roi. Thanks again. Bye-Bye."

Click...

"See? Chairman Le Jour says it's alright."

"Really? That seemed a little glib, didn't it?"

"Oh, no. We go way back, we're pretty tight. I've been planning this for a long time. So, that should settle it, then?"

"I guess so, since you've been planning this, but I don't know?"

"Sure ya do. Things like this happen all the time. Now, before we can do anything, you'll have to sign some papers for me. 'K?"

"Legal crap?"

"Just a few details."

"What do the papers say?"

"Oh, just minor things, like turning all your assets over to me."

"Why is that?"

"So I can pay you!"

"Really? We'll get paid? Finally!"

"Yeah. Did you think that greedy Farnsworth was going to pay you? He's just playing around with your money. If you own it, shouldn't you have it all?"

"Won't that crash the Martian money economy?"

"It might inconvenience a few people. They'll just have to live with it, that's all."

"Gee, ya know, that Farnsworth is real tough. He might get mad. You don't *know* him, Chairman Das Nacht."

"He knows me!"

"*Really?* Well, he gave me an apartment."

"Listen, dear, if you go on this mission, I'll pay you double!"

"Well, you don't have any argument here."

"Okay, then. Before you go, I must test your potential in becoming a Futurist Wizard."

"Aren't we from the future?"

"You most certainly are. I just want to see if you could become a Futurist Wizard for my mission. Think of it as your qualification test, that's all."

"You mean our credentials? That sounds mucho important!"

"It certainly is."

"What will we do when we're a Futurist Wizard?"

"Oh, lots of mechanical stuff that involves motion, speed, and destruction. Essentially, you'll witness your own demise as an esthetic experience. How does that sound?"

"It's sounds real cool, but please translate."

"Think of it as though you were watching a steel robot drowning in a furnace, but only as some cool person from the future living aboard a really neat space ship. Clones, like you, make a perfectly suitable Futurist. It simply comes with the territory."

"Well, been there done that aboard the C.L.O.D. orbiter, but we crashed it."

"I know. You were really good, that's why I chose you guys!"

"Chairman Das Nacht? I don't think you know us very well. I think you've had too many Martian Sunrises."

"Not at all. You won't have to do much of anything. In fact, I imagine all of you sitting around, watching television all day. You'll be able to stay up as late as you want, have the best recordings, and eat as many snacks as you want. Sounds good?"

"Hey, I think I can speak for all of us when I say... We're on board for that!"

"Are we gonna qualify to be a future wizard now?"

"Yes. Let's start with the preliminary tests. They're quite harmless. Shall we begin?"

"Let's do it!"

"Okay. In this first test, I'll examine your Random Psychic ability. I'll show you all a series of cards. Try to guess, I mean, psychically view, what the image is, without seeing it. I know you've done this before at the Institute. I'll record your responses. Okay, ready? Here is the first card..."

"I see a window with a really cool view, a funny robot coffee maker, an old xerox machine, some goofy mutant plants..."

"Hold it, Van! Stop looking around my office. Focus on the card! Okay? Let's start again, only with Numan this time. Numan?"

"Cool! I guess a glazed doughnut, no, how 'bout a weird snake biting its tail!"

"That's good! Susan?"

"I guess my belly button. Are you trying to flirt with me?"

"Van's turn. Try to focus on the card. Van?"

"I like what everybody else said, so, I see a 705 energy bar!"

"Well, you were all close. See? The symbol on the card is a circle. Let's try another one. Numan? You go first again..."

"This is fun! I get it. In my mind, I see a fluffy pillow."

"Okay. Susan?"

"I guess my box. No, wait! I mean, my rover's starting lever."

"Van?"

"I am getting hungry, sooo, I see a 705 *chocolate* energy bar!"

"Alright then, you all did better that time. The card symbol is a square. Here's the next one..."

"Okay, this one is eeeaassy! I see a slice of blackberry pie!"

"Susan?"

"Oh, wait! It's coming to me... Oh, I guess an Earth house in the country. No, wait, a man's beard. No, how 'bout an opened Chinese fan? Why do I see lots of things? It's hard to make up my mind."

"You only have one choice with your answer, Susan."

"All right then. It's my rack, from the side."

"Good choice. It's your turn, Van."

"Okay, now I see a 705 vanilla/chocolate energy bar, but I can't decide which one, either."

"That was O.K. You all did O.K. The symbol on the card is a triangle. Alright? Here is the last card. Please try your best..."

"This is a hard one. I guess... Smoke?"

"And Susan?"

"Oh, I saw this one right away. I saw my... *Geez*, you're really getting personal with me, Chairman Das Nacht. You better control yourself. I think you have a dirty mind. I kinda like that."

"Dear, it's only a card! For heaven's sake, focus on the card!"

"Okay, okay. Don't get mad at me. I am trying my best. Alright, I guess the image is my hairy... I mean, my hair, on my *head*, that is."

"Susan, you're a piece of work, you know?... Go ahead, Van, last card..."

"I was so hungry that I had it all to myself and didn't share. I couldn't help myself. All I see now is a - 705 vanilla/chocolate energy bar - Wrapper!"

"Very good, guys – on that last one. The card symbol is three horizontal wavy lines. Now let me take a moment and I'll give you your test results. Let's see, here. Ahmm, carry the 2, with the 1 left over. Divided by... O.K., Numan and Susan each get one point, and Van gets 20 points."

"Hey! Wait a minute, Chairman *Does Not!* Why should Susan and I get lower scores than Van? We guessed things that were in the shape of those symbols and Van kept guessing only one thing!"

"Cool it, cool it. You and Susan guessed similar Random things. You were all over the place. Van wasn't in the ball park as far as similarities go. As a matter of fact, he wasn't even in the same city, but Van's images became actual to him. Eventually, he would have guessed it. You should thank him because his score qualified all of you to go on to the next round. Congratulations!"

"Alright, *Van*! We's qualified."

"Yeah, dude. Gimme five up high - too slow for you!"

"Now, we will test your emotional empathy."

"What does that mean? It sounds way too hard."

"It might be. You all have a tendency to get confused. All you care about is yourselves. You get so wrapped up and become paralyzed when confronted with stress. You become unable to speak and ask questions when you're afraid. So, really try to give good answers this time. This is a test to see how you care about someone else."

"Is it like the last test? I mean, harmless?"

"Somewhat. I'll tell you a story."

"Oh, I hope it's not too long. We really get annoyed when it doesn't make any sense."

"Yeah, dude. Can we ask questions during the story?"

"No. I just want you to tell me how you feel. It's that easy."

"How we feel about what?"

"Just how you feel about what happens in the story, Van."

"Am I in the story?"

"Nooo!"

"Then how can I tell you how I feel?"

"I want you to tell me how you feel about the people in the story. Okay? It's not that hard."

"Hey, I *know*. You want me to tell you if the story is sad, or happy, or wonderful, or scarey..."

"That's close, Susan, but it's not about the story, it's how you feel about..."

"See, I know what. I was a sad and lonely story, once. It scared me when I lost my dancing job, but then I got discovered at a wonderful bar. My Clone Dome values have been *dramatically* altered, I can chit-chat on the phone now, so I'm happy – like this story."

"You are really something, girl, but let's get on with it. You'll see what you have to do."

"I thought all I'll have to do is think about the story."

"Numan, *you will*. I am losing it with you. Can't you just cooperate?"

"Don't get all tight, Mister Chairman. I can go with the flow!"

"Hey, that's good. You just showed me how you feel. Keep doing that throughout the story. Now, listen closely: A man paced anxiously around the emergency waiting room at the hospital. His wife had given birth and he was, naturally, worried about her and the child. He was waiting a long time to hear from the doctor..."

"Is this the story, now? 'Cause this is scary!"

"Please listen to the rest. O.K.? The doctor finally came in and said to him, your wife is fine, she pulled through the delivery just fine. The man cried, that's a relief, I was so worried about her. I love her so, but what about my son? How is he? Well, you see, answered the doctor, very concerned, we really don't know if it's a boy or a girl. That's O.K., the man said, we could live with that. We'll buy it gender neutral diapers. Well, that's not quite all of it, said the doctor, your baby was born without arms or legs. That's O.K., said the man, we'll still love it and carry it around. We'll still sing lullabies and talk baby talk to it. Geez, I don't think so, answered the doctor, it was born without ears. What could be worse than that? the man exclaimed. It was born without a mouth, the doctor answered. What could be worse than that?, the man said. I think you should come and see, said the doctor. They walked into the delivery room and saw a big, blood-shot, eyeball laying in the crib..."

"That would have frighten me. I would have ran right out of that hospital. What could be worse than having an eyeball for a kid!"

"It's blind."

"Ouchy! What could be worse than that, Chairman Das Nacht?"

"Someone stole it."

"Yikes! Why would they do that?"

"They used it as a volleyball."

"Zowie! That's a crappy ball to play with. It wouldn't bounce."

"They spiked it out of bounds."

"Ooops! That's awful – lose a serve. What could be worse than that?"

"They lost the game."

"Bummer! Nothing's that bogus."

"They had to play on the road."

"Eeeks! In a scuzzy hotel room? What could be more downer than that?"

"They called Missing Persons."

"Zoinks! What could be... No, wait! That isn't... Uh, what could be worse than that? Was that good?"

"They took it away from the team."

"Yowza! How are they gonna play now. This is confusing! What could be worse than that?!"

"They brought it back to the hospital."

"Gadzooks! That's good, no, could anything get better or worse than that?"

"It's your baby!"

"Yuck! Chairman Das Nacht? That was confusing. We didn't know what to do. What does this all mean?"

"It means, you have to take responsibility for your actions, and do the best you can. Tests are over. You've all qualified. Off you go!"

"You mean we get to go back on vacation?"

"No, you get to go on the *space ship*. It's parked out back. Your mission awaits! See ya, later!"

"Wait. What mission?"

"The mission I've been preparing you for all along, when we trained you to work in the C.L.O.D. orbiter, and now with these tests."

"How long will this mission take? We gotta get going back to – ahhh, Susan's apartment."

"Oh, give or take, a couple of light years."

"Gee, that's not too bad. We can do a couple of years, and then come back for vacation."

"So, ah, Chairman Das Nacht? What are we gonna do on this mission, again?"

"Well, you're gonna blast off on a long trip, but forget about all of that suspended animation nonsense. That crap never worked. You'll have to suck it up and live it out. Try not to get too bored. Sit around, really get to know each other, have a few laughs, play some pool or shuffle board. The best part of it, is you'll get to have babies – lots of them!"

"We get to have sex with Susan? Finally!"

"If I may, can I have a word in edgewise here?"

"Go ahead, Susan."

"Gee, I can flirt with the best of them, but I am not too sure about having babies yet. I don't know if I've ever been *asked* to babysit. I've only petted a mangy dog in the Pleasure Colony zoo!"

"You may not feel like it now, but you will. As time passes, you'll get very promiscuous and just plain horny. Because you passed the empathy test, we know you'll take care of your babies. It's important to pass that knowledge along, during your long voyage."

"So, where are we going, on this year long mission?"

"I'm aiming your ship towards Epsilon Geminorum. It's a star in the Gemini constellation. You'll find a little planet there, that's not too hot, and not too cold. It's just right."

"You mean this will be a comfortable little Earth?"

"Sure! We even think there's an alien race living there. They'll somehow signal to you, when you get close."

"We get to party with some cool alien dudes? Right on!"

"Yeah. We hope so. We're sending some stuff with you – things they might need."

"How do you know aliens live there?"

"We found remnants of their civilization in the Chinese territory, by the Cangwu crater. This showed us where they're located. We pointed signals at their planet, but they won't answer our calls. We always get a busy signal. That means it's a popular planet."

"Saaay! What he's saying might be true. The fortune teller said I'd meet some handsome strangers."

"How did you contact them?"

"I've got news for you. Your Clone Domes really aren't signaling devices to keep track of you at all. By linking all the Clone Domes together, it really creates a huge signal and receiving dish. It constantly sends out signals and receives them from Epsilon. We thought we heard a blip, which we thought was like a message. It all added up, so I'm banking on that."

"How will we be able to talk with these alien dudes, once we get to party down?"

"That's a good question, Van. I am so glad you asked that. Well, you know your Random Thought implants? That enable you to speak like a human?"

"Sure do! It always crosses my mind."

"Well, a long time ago, I created a data base that stores all the euphemisms, vernacular, and slang in the human language. We found that clones had a hard time with specificity. So, we gave them implants with this data base, to help them express their thoughts easier. However, when this Epsilon thing emerged, I was able to hack, I mean, get into the data base and create a program that will translate your language into theirs. The robot program will automatically download when you get there. You'll be able to speak their language with no problem once you meet them. Your children will have easy, do-it-yourself instructions on how to apply this. It will be like taking a chill pill."

"What do you think these alien dudes look like? Are they cool?"

"From what I know, they're stand-offish, shy, and nervous. They're kinda like squirrels, only I've never seen a squirrel, since they're extinct. But that's the beauty of it! By the time you'll meet them, your descendants will have devolved into cretins, and the aliens will have evolved into Neanderthals. They'll be quite compatible together, actually."

"Chairman Das Nacht? You said that we'll be taking some stuff with us. What's with that?"

"Oh, you'll take lots of stuff."

"Hey, Van. We's packing!"

"Yeah, are we packing lots of goodies?"

"Yes, I made sure of that. Mostly hybrid stuff: a little basalt, some carpet remnants, Mr Bunny plastic rulers, some rubber erasers... We think they'll evolve far enough to make different kinds of ketchup and mustard, but we don't know for sure if they invented mayonnaise. So, we're sending varieties of Thousand Island dressing, in hopes, that they'll learn how to combine things. After they go through it all, making sandwiches, we hope they'll reciprocate on some level 'cause that's the polite thing to do."

"You'll want them to signal back?"

"All we want is a thank you."

"Boy, this space ship sounds quite roomy, if we's packing all that."

"Ah, not really. Unfortunately, you'll have to move around a lot of boxes to get from one module to another. We had to save on energy costs."

"How is this thing gonna get there?"

"Well, space is rather a messy place. There's lots of trash out there. So, we made the ship similar to the C.L.O.D. orbiter, but instead of sending the debris down to Mars, it collects it for fuel. If that should run out, there's a reactor on board that burns dark matter."

"What's dark matter?"

"Oh, that's matter you can't see. It's the exhaust matter expelled from high energy. It's quite exhausted, but it burns cleaner than space debris. You'll never run out of that stuff."

"Is it like antimatter?"

"No, that doesn't exist – what do you think this is, Science Fiction?"

"So, is that why you chose us for this mission? Because we served on the C.L.O.D. orbiter?"

"Precisely. After I lost my assistant, Toby, to a most unfortunate training mishap, I had to look around for a replacement. General George Keith highly recommended you to me, after he came back from his permanent vacation. I sent Sharon out to find you. So, here you are! It's getting late, guys. You should really settle into your new digs. I have to get ready for my party tomorrow. Lots to do. This is the first year my tarot card design won. I want to celebrate with a bang. Your blast-off will be the icing on the cake!"

"Chairman Das Nacht? Gee, thanks for letting us be part of your party and all, but aren't you forgetting one thing?"

"What's that, Numan?"

"Where do we change clothes for our mission?"

"Oh?... Uh, just wear the paper uniforms that are issued aboard the ship."

"One more thing, Chairman?"

"Yes, what's that?"

"Where do we take a shower? We like to be clean."

"You can do that anytime aboard the ship."

"Oh, goody! Does it have lots of settings?"

"I think you'll find it quite adequate."

"Is the medicine cabinet stocked with all our strong medicines and essential oils?"

"I think I knew what you needed. It's all there."

"Is there water on this planet?"

"We think, by the best estimations, that there is some water. Yes."

"How much? I want to royally shred some tubes."

"I don't know if you'll be able to do that. However, it's likely there will be lots of ice. You could always melt it down. I suppose."

"Say, what are the aliens called? We want to be like Bros."

"For now, we call them Xitlan."

"What does that mean? Is it personal?"

"It's from an Aztec word meaning; near the stars."

"So, we're all gonna be like stars?"

"Yeah, you came from the stars, in a manner of speaking."

"Alright! How far away is Xitlan, again?"

"Some light years from here. Look, all these Random Scientific questions of yours are giving me a headache. I want to get the decorations for my party ordered. It's going to take me a lot of time to decide what kind of cake I want. The frosting alone could..."

"Where are we going again?"

"To Xitan, for the last time."

"No, Chairman Das Nacht, I think what Van means is; where do we go to get into our cool new space ship?"

"Oh, that's all? It's parked out back. Just go down the hall and follow the black line to the ramp. It's right there."

"This hall?"

"Yep. Happy landing. See ya later."

"Thanks for everything, Chairman, dude. It was fun learning about ice and dark matter. Now, I can't wait to do this mission, so we can get back to our vacation."

"Alright! Lets get going, guys."

"Yeah, I want to crawl aboard that ship and take a long shower. I feel all yucky from that office."

"Thumb wrestle for it, Susan!"

"No way. I called it first."

"Well, you always get to go first. Why can't you let me go first for once..."

"*Daddy?!*"

"Huh, whaa? Sharon?"

"Daddy? *Stop it!*"

"What? Dearie. *Honey pie?*"

"These are my friends!"

"So?"

"*So!* You were going to send them on a *stupid mission* to Xitlan, weren't you?"

"Well, I guess I was..."

"Call them back right now, or I won't move into the new penthouse you bought for me!"

"But I've been planning this for so long! I had to kick out all the First Generation clones on the waiting list for that penthouse for you. I had it decorated exactly like you wanted it. Don't do this, butter cup!"

"Call them back, or I'll won't go to the party tomorrow."

"Geez! Now that's hitting below the belt. Do I have to?"

"Call them back and apologize to them, right now!"

"Dang it! You're just like your mother sometimes. You always seem to find a way right when, I get a party started. Oh, alright! ...*Van,*

Numan, and Susan, please report to my office, pronto..."

"This is so awkward! Why do you always put me in an awkward position? What were you thinking, Daddy? You always come so close. So close! Then you do this Xitlan thing and it never works out. Why can't you just be, for just once...? Oh, you give me such *distress* all the time. I could call Mommy anytime, and go to live with her. I know you wouldn't like it. At least, she would be there, but you always come so close. So close! This is sooo awkward..."

"Sharon, Baaaby. Can we talk about this later? I can hear your friends coming up the ramp, they might overhear us. Try not to make a scene. Okay?"

"Hi, Guys!"

"Hi, Sharon."

"Hi, Sharon. What are you doing here?"

"Oh Van, I was looking all over for you after I got out of the shower."

"You mean you were on the space ship already?"

"No, I thought you got lost after taking out the trash. That was the most thoughtful thing anyone has ever done for me. I waited a long time for you to come back. I thought you got lost, so I came looking for you."

"Well, I waited by the door for a while, hollering; we went to see the fortune teller. She scared us, but she told Susan things, that were the same things as other things, and somehow, I got locked out."

"Normally, I always leave the door unlocked, but when my dad comes over, he puts it on auto-lock when he leaves."

"Daddy? Were you over at my place this afternoon?"

"Oh yeah, I forgot. I had to pick up my Yi Jing chart. I hope you don't mind. I took a few facial lotions and some of your tea and flour, okay?"

"You guys? My daddy has something important to say to you."

"Locking the door isn't a big deal, Sharon. It's okay."

"No, Van, it's not just that. It's about the mission. He has something to say about the mission. Daddy? I am waiting..."

"Alright then! I am sorry for sending your friends on a mission! Excuse me for living! I can't help my habit of auto-locking the door. Satisfied? Can I go now? Frosting the cake is a complicated thing. There is butter or cream, or butter cream, or yogurt or tofu, or yogurt tofu..."

"I'll clear this up with you later, Daddy. We'll discuss it over lunch after your party tomorrow, okay?"

"Whatever. See you then, honey bun kisses. Good day everyone..."

"Sharon? I was wondering? Why was your dad all mad when he called us back to apologize? We were going to meet this cool alien race, and felt weird, seeing things on card in our minds, but we qualified to be Futurist Wizards and everything."

"Every time I hang out with someone, my dad always seems to find a way to get rid of them."

"No way!"

"Yep! My last boyfriend, Toby, was my dad's assistant. When he found out we were getting serious, he asked Toby to volunteer for the mission to Xitlan. Toby declined after he found out that my dad was looking into insurance policies. Not long after this, he got rid of him. "

"He got rid of Toby too!"

"I admit that Toby was a real ding bat, but he *was* always good for a few laughs. He was the closest human to a Seventh Generation clone my dad could find. After he fired him, he had to look around for somebody else. He found out that you guys came back to Mars on vacation. So, he chose you. You were going to be Toby's replacement. Oh, I wish I hadn't brought you here."

"Yikes! What could be worse than that?"

"This is a stupid mission my dad thought up."

"Ouchy! What could be worse than that?"

"Ever since the Chinese found some weird fossil bones, my dad has got it in his head that there's an alien race out there. The Chinese were really digging around an old garbage dump, and found some chicken bones and NASA trash. They claimed they discovered alien fossils, and put them in their Museum of Natural History. After they realized it was trash, they tried to destroyed it in order to cover it up. Some moron managed to save parts of the chicken bones, and put them in the display case next to *real* pieces of Thor's Hammer. This nutty story still lives on, and the Institute uses it, in their random covert war to misguide and tease the Chinese. Everybody else knows except my dad! He really embarrasses me at times."

"What about our becoming Futurist Wizards. Wasn't that true?"

"My dad was simply asking you to sacrifice yourselves for the mission. Do you like the idea of dying on that ship?"

"No way, Ho-zay!"

"Well that's what would have happened. It would have taken generations to get there. Your descendants wouldn't have found any aliens on this knucklehead planet. You would have died on that ship. It was never coming back!"

"Gadzooks! This changes everything. I really wanted to be some kind of neat Wizard."

"You guys are my friends. I couldn't let you go there."

"Gee, Sharon, thanks for saving us. We didn't want to die on that crummy ship. Can I give you a hug!"

"Maybe later, but unfortunately, you still have to go on the mission. You'll have to leave right now."

"Excuse me?"

"Next week, I'm opening up a new Martian surplus store on Earth and I really need you to deliver my supplies."

"You mean we have to go on that crummy ship again?"

"Hey, don't sweat it, sweetheart! I had Giovanni, my best interior decorator re-do the entire living compartments. He really has good taste in accessories. You'll have the latest. If I know Giovanni, it will be swank! Also, the ship will be more roomy. It won't be so cramped because I replaced my dad's crappy stuff with my own designer fabrics."

"Can I ask where on Earth is this surplus store?"

"Sure! They just opened a new Pleasure Colony in the most fashionable part of Paris. My store will be right next to it. We did a lot of market research, and we found that Parisians love Martian fashion, 'cause we don't do anything. I'll probably fly down later this year to see how Giovanni set it up. I also had him find a nice apartment for you near the store."

"How are we gonna be able to speak the French lingo?"

"That was one thing my dad got right. The alien translator program he created for your Random Thought implants includes all the languages. He knew that the French are really stubborn and particular when it comes to their language. So, he made damn sure it was included. All the instructions for downloading it are on the ship. You'll be speaking French as though you were born there."

"I think I've heard of this program, Sharon. Isn't it just a little robot pill?"

"Yes it is. I can tell by the way Van and Numan speak that they took one a long time ago."

"Is that the reason why they talk, you know, so affected?"

"It could be, but something isn't quite right. When General George Keith sent you guys to Earth, did you take the entire translator pill?"

"No. We split one 'cause we were scared!"

"Oh, that explains it then. If you would've taken the entire pill, you'd be speaking fluent surfer dude vernacular. Instead, your speech is more Southern California suburban than actual Malibu."

"Well, *duh!*"

"So, I'll give you the choice. Who wants to go?""

"That sounds good to me, Sharon. I was thinking I wanted to see some green trees and lakes again."

"What about you, Susan?"

"Sure! Paris sounds quite romantic. Besides, I could never really tell the difference between Van and Numan, and the fortune teller *did* tell me my long journey would be interrupted. And she was right! Oh, I forgot. What about my job at Chairman Le Jour's office and the typing competition?"

"Don't worry about that. I advised Roi to hire the girl from the ESP office. She'll win the typing competition for you."

"You thought of everything, Sharon. You go, girl!"

"Well, if everyone's going, I want to go too."

"Sorry, Van. Space and time laws allow for only two. That means you're out."

"Dang it!"

"Listen, I would love for you to be with your friends and all, but the first law of the Castor Pollux space/time principle says that you have to alternate your position with Susan and Numan. When they go to Earth, you have to be on Mars, and so on. You'll never be able to be in the same place together."

"What does that mean, Sharon?"

"It's kinda like when Seventh Generation clones go to the Zenith. Only two can thrash on the dance floor at the same time with the First Generations. All the others must wait their turn at the bar, or else there would be a major mosh pit. That's how you and Numan landed on Earth a long time ago."

"But what about Clone Officer Susan? The three of us came back to Mars, 'member?"

"Oh, that? She's a First Generation Pleasure clone and was able to withstand the journey back. The three of you are Seventh Generation clones, and three can't go into two."

"I guess it doesn't add up then?"

"You guys have better get going. You can always chat later through the inter-space web."

"You mean, we can still talk to each other, even though we're using the same Castor Pollux communicator?"

"Yes, remember? You just can't be physically in the same room together, and besides that, they will have to learn English all over again or you'll have to learn French. You'll find out who's the most stubborn. You have thirty minutes now, so say your good-byes in English and then off you go."

"See ya later, Susan. Be good to Numan. He shall always be my Clone Bro."

"Are you flirting with me?"

"Numan? Keep it real."

"Keep it real, Van."

"As real as it gets, dude. Late-trey!"

"Lets get going, Susan. Last one there is a rotten egg. Do you think we can take a shower together, like, right after we take off?"

"Showers are kinda like a riddle. The spring rain setting is different than the ultra-light snowflake setting, and la brume jardin est plus agreable que la pluie d'automne...."

"Well, Sharon, I'll see you whenever. I want to chillax at the Zenith bar and grill. I think I need a drink."

"Not so fast, Van."

"What's up?"

"I still have business with you."

"You want to fool around?"

"Maybe? I have something in mind for you, starting tomorrow."

"What's that?"

"After Toby left me, there's new a job opening. The position is *my* assistant boy toy. Do you want to apply?"

"Does this mean I'll be your boyfriend?"

"Nooo. I could never marry a clone. Sorry about that. Can we still be friends?"

"I guess a boy toy is way cooler than a robot maid. Who needs a fortune teller to tell me what would work out, any way?"

"Here's the key card to my apartment. Don't worry about my dad auto-locking the door. Use whatever food, clothes, lotions, or anything else that's there. It's all yours now. I am going to live in a new penthouse my dad bought me on the top floor."

"What will I do as your boy toy assistant?"

"You'll sit around the pool, and swim whenever you want. You'll work on various kinds of leisure with me. Your main duty will be to advise me on which dress or outfit I should wear, and what looks good on me. We'll do lots of shopping together. I may call you at any hour, so you'll have to be available at all times – that's the booty call boy toy part of your job. Sounds good?"

"That's awesome!"

"Then you'll start tomorrow. I'll need your help to choose the right dress for my daddy's party. And now, that I made the appointment with him for lunch, I'll need a change of clothes. You'll have to approve another dress for me. I don't want to look stale."

"Sounds real fresh!"

"Alright then, our business here is done. See you bright and early at my penthouse. Try not to get too shit-faced at the bar tonight. I don't want you to be too Random, picking out a dress. I gotta run and check the decorations for the party. I suppose my daddy is still trying to decide what frosting he wants. He's terrible at these things. He always comes so close, so close..."

"Schlater, Sharon..."

"Good evening, sir. Can I help you find what you'd like?"

"Wow, what a crazy bar this is! Hey fella! Would you mind moving over one? I like this chair."

"Knock yourself out, dude."

"Hey, Metal Bartender, why is there a naked girl standing next to me?"

"That's my new bar maid, Suzie. I hired her last week. She's quite a People Pleaser, isn't she?"

"Well, she's certainly not hung up. I guess I really don't understand these new fashions, where everyone doesn't have to do anything."

"Affirmative, sir. It's all a designer look. Notice how the thin, black ribbon, around her neck drapes down, to tie it all together. It's the new thing in comfort we're trying out this spring. We want to make sure our employees feel right at home."

"Well, they certainly perk out at me. So, hey, little machine 'tender. What shall I consume tonight?"

"Affirmative. It depends on what you'd like."

"I don't know what I like. There are so many varieties to choose from – so many choices. I think I need something strong in chemicals."

"Affirmative. May I suggest a Martian Sunrise? It packs a wallop and has less calories than our regular Sunrise."

"Sounds good."

"May I ask why you need a liquid punch in the face?"

"Well, I'm no longer loaded on vacation."

"Negative. We all can't be loaded, all the time."

"I qualified to be a Future Wizard, and then found out that I couldn't."

"Affirmative. Wizards are a dime a dozen."

"Then I had to ditch my rover 'cause the engine light came on."

"Affirmative. Red rover, red rover, let the Martian Sunrise take over."

"Now, I'm a boy toy, picking out dresses to wear!"

"Affirmative. I was programmed to have good taste in fashion. I love all colors and textures. I could help you with that, Madam."

"Wait. Is that you, Puter?"

"Affirmative. My booze hound activation system tells me it's you, Van."

"It sure is, dude. Can you turn on your Visual Sensory panel?"

"It's been a while, it's kinda blurry from all the splash, but I can see you now. Greetings, Van."

"We thought we left you at the restaurant on Earth."

"Affirmative. My strong magnetic tracking system pulled me along with your ship. It was quite a hairy ride back to Mars."

"Where did you end up?"

"They put me on a conveyor belt in the Module dump area 502. I was downloaded so far that it looked like up to me. My file functions remained intact. I was able to save a large file of Earth cocktail recipes, so they connected me here."

"I guess you feel right at home, then."

"Affirmative. Very useful. Where is Numan?"

"He went back to Earth to see some green trees and lakes with Susan."

"Typical Earth girl, Susan?"

"No."

"Suzette Susan?

"No."

"Clone Officer Susan, Susan?"

"No."

"Bar maid Suzie, Susan?"

"Nooo."

"My Susan data base is quite extensive. We could be here all night."

"Susan Dix or Miss Dix or Susan Dixon or *Susan*..."

"Affirmative. Let me look her up here... Ahhh. She's quite a doll, a Seventh Generation clone, from the Gusev Pleasure Colony, to boot. Quite adequate for either of you."

"Well, she didn't know she went with Numan. They speak French.

They left me all alone. They went to Paris and my girlfriend can't go along, either. We have to change the dance floors. I lost everything."

"Affirmative. I can sense that you did. I tried to warn you."

"When did you do that?"

"When you and Numan were drinking with Chairman Das Nacht. I sent a message in the bottom of your glass."

"What did it say?"

"'Member? It said, Leave Now!"

"So, you were the one!"

"Chairman Das Nacht is a dangerous cat. He's always throwing out these goofy ideas at everyone. He was going to send me on the mission with you, but I wanted to stay here. My sensory panels can't take zero gravity any more – some parts are hanging. When I sensed that you were with him, I tried to warn you, but you didn't listen."

"Wow, Puter. You saved me when the C.L.O.D. orbiter was shutting down, you tried to save me from the mission, and now, you offered to help me pick out dresses. You are my only true friend. You've been there all along."

"Affirmative. Just doing my job."

"Could we be best Buds?"

"Negative. I am a bartender, not a waiter."

"Could we be best Bros?"

"Negative. I am a computer, not a robot."

"Could you be my assistant?"

"I may be pliant, but I'm not fragile."

"Well, come on then, Puter. I have something to show you."

"My shift!... Hey Charlie? Be back later..."

"Well, what do you think?"

"Oh, my god! Oh, my god!"

"It's all yours, Puter. I hope you're pleased."

"That is awesome!"

"I hope you like it."

"This is for me?"

"Yep, it's all yours. Take a look around. Check it out."

"Affirmative. Look at all these rugs, these plants, and pictures?! It even has a glass patio! This is living large. I could totally live here."

"I knew you could. They make you connect yourself to the outlet under the sink, don't they?"

"The towel cabinet is quite an inadequate off chamber."

"Look in here, Puter."

"You bought me my own robot maid?"

"Yep, pure plastic!"

"You are the best Van ever."

"I always extra-sensed that I was. So, let's chill by the solar fire place, have a few laughs, and talk about old times over drinks. Shall we?"

"Affirmative!"

"Puter? I've always wanted to tell you how lovely your panels reflect in the starlight."

"Oh, why thank you, but I think I have something to tell you about my past."

"What's that, my little machine 'tender?"

"For a long time, I was connected to another hard drive. Actually, it was just a cheap flash drive. I'm so ashamed. I tried saving all my files to download at the right time."

"That's okay, I am sure it was just a flash in the panels."

"So you don't mind that I interfaced with a cute game console, on a

LAN system, all those years?"

"Hey, life goes on. One thing I learned as a Futurist Wizard, eventually, I'd get it."

"Affirmative."

End

Made in the USA
Charleston, SC
25 June 2013